T0128136

ROCKS IN
TREES

RONALD L. CLARK

iUniverse

ROCKS IN TREES

iUniverse books may be ordered through booksellers or by contacting:

iUniverse
1663 Liberty Drive
Bloomington, IN 47403
www.iuniverse.com
1-800-Authors (1-800-288-4677)

ISBN: 978-1-5320-1356-0 (sc)
ISBN: 978-1-5320-1355-3 (e)

Library of Congress Control Number: 2017900517

Print information available on the last page.

iUniverse rev. date: 01/17/2017

Other Books by Ronald L. Clark

The Grace of Being

Flim Flam

I'm Just Saying

Libertas and Thunderbolt

Contents

PREFACE

One day in the land that occupies the space between the coasts, my television set became nonfunctional. This inconvenient dysfunction was not due to a technical failure of the various well-designed electronic parts that make up a modern television, but the blank screen was more likely due to nonpayment to an unsympathetic and uncaring cable company. To further compound the loneliness caused by this absence, I attempted to replace the normal mind-numbing and comforting TV offerings by trying to engage my social brethren in some equally insipid political discussions.

Big mistake.

My normal football-watching buddies were also unsympathetic and uncaring to my plight. My so-called buddies not only avoided eye contact with me but ran for the nearest escape routes when I attempted to provide a suitable provocative subject for political discussion.

So in utter desperation, I decided to meander down to Brown County, Indiana, not only because it's a convenient, beautiful, and primal locale in south central Indiana but because, I reasoned, lollygagging around beautiful Brown County would be a fine substitute for mind-numbing TV and provocative political discussions.

Yes, indeed, for once, this was a really inspired decision that could expand my mind and increase my total awareness by allowing me to view and interact with inspirational nature in its pure and natural setting. This had to be better than destroying brain cells by watching network TV or alienating casual friends by trying to put lipstick on Democratic and Republican political policies and positions.

So I fired up my blow smoke Chevy heap and headed on down to Brown County. As I got under way, the roar of the revving V-8 engine seemed to sync with my flagging spirit, which gave me cause to rev up my TV-numbed mojo. This was starting to get exciting. As I sped along, my spirit was buoyed up, not only because of the roaring engine and thumping road sounds but also because of the notion that I was finally doing something that my more enlightened acquaintances would approve of.

Perhaps I could even be given grudging entrée into the cabal of beautiful people because of my demonstrated nature awareness and newfound Green attitude.

Yes, yes, this little inconvenient but inspired adventure might well provide a good opportunity to expand my social universe with the beautiful people. Plus a rewarding escapade might also be awaiting me in primal environs of scenic Brown County.

With my Detroit belch fire V8 engine thumping along the highway and my CD pumping out music that complemented the roar of the engine, my loud and off-key voice added to the road noise in a spirited rendition of "On the Road Again."

Damn, it's good to be alive and on the road to fine times and high purpose.

But of course, there are always bugs in paradise, and as I was rocking and rolling along, one of those bugs popped up in my sight. The bug came in the form of a Dairy Queen advertising sign on the highway that surely would have caused Lady Bird Johnson to come down with a case of the vapors.

The DQ sign was directly en route to the lands, streams, and forests of beautiful Brown County. Surely there is a reason why the merchant class spend so much money erecting advertising signs in spite of Lady Bird's spirited campaign to rid the curse of highway signs on America's highways.

But of course, the reason why *they* spend big bucks erecting such psychological messages on our highways is because it's really easy to distract a person bent on high purpose by presenting an opportunity for a Death by Chocolate brownie confection.

So yielding to my salivating desires, I slid my indistinguishable Chevy heap into a convenient parking spot at an also indistinguishable Dairy Queen located somewhere between here and there.

After ordering and paying for my sinful extravagance, I watched with abject fascination as a pimply teenager dressed in a clumsy DQ uniform casually forked out a gargantuan fudge-layered brownie as the foundation to my immoral concoction.

The youthful fabricator then added the frozen white stuff called Dairy Queen to the brownie. The frozen white stuff was dispensed upon the fudge-layered brownie with a measure of artistry—a series of spiral shapes that further invoked involuntary (Pavlov's dog) onrush of salivation in me.

Not bothering to even look up at me, he then shuffled along rows of dispensing nozzles until he found the right one. Then he pressed it, and heavy chocolate guck oozed down all over my DQ white stuff. The awkward youth then slid the object of my gastronomical desire over the counter to me.

I carefully picked it up.

I looked at my without-any-socially-redeeming-qualities confection with great devotion and much anticipation while locating an out-of-the-way table where I could indulge guilt-free. As I sat down, I happened to look over at another out-of-the-way table where a local yokel was making tasty love to the latest DQ Blizzard.

Mr. Local Yokel glanced up at me during a lip-smacking interval, and with multicolored sprinkles dribbling down from his lips, he smiled and nodded his approval at my overflowing calorie bomb.

The stranger's unsolicited and expert approval caused a wave of satisfaction to spring up within me. This, in turn, produced an immediate bond with my fellow DQer.

DQ protocol demanded that I wait until the local yokel had finished his confection before I responded and struck up a conversation. So after the proper delay was observed, I casually walked over to my DQ brother and introduced myself. After the perfunctory exchanging of salutations was completed, I explained I was down in Brown County to enjoy the splendor of the place after exiting the dehumanizing big city.

Mr. Local Yokel immediately inquired, "Are you down from Indianapolis?"

Embarrassed, with downcast eyes, I admitted I was indeed an Indy urbanite and had escaped the urban sprawl to find spiritual renewal in the beautiful expanse of the Brown County environs.

Mr. Local Yokel squinted his puffy, watery eyes and replied, "You think Brown County is a beautiful place where you can find peace and harmony to renew your busted big-city spirit?"

My face returned to its normal cheerful and enthusiastic look as I hurried to reply, "Well, yes."

Mr. Local Yokel stifled an impolite chuckle, shifted his position in his chair with much great effort, cleared his throat, and said, "Well now, I don't know much about renewing spirits other than with a stiff shot of Old Grand Dad, but if you're looking to find something unusual around these parts, I suggest you go over to Needmore and go look at that rock stuck up in that tree."

I inquired, "Are you saying there is a rock stuck up in a tree around here? What's that all about?"

Mr. Local Yokel struck a confident pose and said with a hushed voice that was better suited to calling hogs, "There are those around here that say there is evidence that aliens from outer space visited here. They say that because in the Yellowwood State Forest, just outside of Needmore, Indiana, there is a tall oak tree on the banks of Plum Crick that has this huge rock stuck in its upper reaches. That big rock is stuck up in that tree and is wedged in a fork that is more than eighty feet off the ground."

Warming up to his subject, Mr. Local Yokel carried on, "No one can figure out how that big of a rock got put up into that tree, so it seems reasonable to most folks around these parts that space people and their spaceships were somehow responsible for a 650-pound rock getting itself stuck up in a tree in the middle of nowhere."

"You know," he said while looking around to see if others were listening, "there have been lots of strange things going on around here lately. Most people around these parts think there is another Roswell brewing right here in the middle of Brown County."

I was absolutely stunned by the revelation.

Well now, vegetating in front of a TV and mutilating brain cells is one thing, but looking at a potential full-scale adventure is quite another. So with much anticipation, I asked the knowledgeable Hoosier for directions to the place where you could find evidence of this otherworldly event.

Mr. Local Yokel seemed to radiate a smug satisfaction when he rubbed his unshaven face and proclaimed, "I'll be happy to tell you where to go. First, get on down to Needmore, which is about twenty minutes south of here."

With some curious pondering, I noted that Mr. Local Yokel measured distance by saying how much time it would be required to get there. Even though I am a Hoosier by birth, perhaps my engineering training compels me to consider the metrics of differing modes of travel to be more accurate than only considering the time required to get to a destination. *Oh well*, I thought, *it must be one of those down-home Hoosier things that doesn't consider exactness to be all that important during everyday activity.*

But he did say Needmore, Indiana, right?

Yeah, that was right—*Needmore, Indiana.*

Wouldn't you just love to find out how the tiny town of Needmore got its name? Maybe during the process of naming their new community, the more prosaic of the down-home folk insisted that they first address what they needed more of before they could become a real town. Us modern folk can only speculate as to what the stout Hoosier pioneers felt they needed more of in order to become a proper town. Did they need more women? Did they need more comely women? Did they need more money? Did they need more food? Did they need more space? Did they need more water? Did they need more suitable land that could actually be farmed? Did they need more peace? Did they need more religion? Did they need more honest men? Did they need more men willing to work hard? Did they need more men who at least looked good?

And thus, it may well have finally occurred to the gentle folk trying to name their place in the sun that they should give their town the interim name of Needmore until such a time as they finally got what it was that they needed more of. And then after they finally got what they felt they needed, they could then give their brand-new town a proper name befitting the people living there.

Sounded reasonable and righteous to most folks, Hoosier or not.

And thus, it would further appear that they never got what they thought they needed more of because the tiny town still bears the name Needmore to this very day.

All in all, this would seem to authenticate the Hoosier way of doing things.

The real Hoosiers who probably knew how the town of Needmore got its name were long gone by now. And besides, even if there were some of those Hoosiers still around, they would not give up the answer straight away anyway.

Why?

Well, real down-home Hoosiers rarely entertain the necessity to blab the truth, the whole truth, and nothing but the truth to strangers. That was why.

But wait. There's more.

There is also a tiny town named Gnaw Bone located just a few miles from the town of Needmore. Perhaps some of the Needmore people became disappointed and disillusioned with the whole Needmore enterprise and just moved on. And so perhaps the restless Needmorians shuffled off to where Gnaw Bone is now located to see if they could at least find a little of what they felt they needed more of.

However, the town name, Gnaw Bone, suggests to me and others the possible relocation and search for whatever they needed more of did not end well. After all, if the town name of Gnaw Bone was meant to convey the reality of the people who lived there and those who did live there had to gnaw on bones to survive, then the American dream of eating well and often was not only absent in Gnaw Bone, Indiana, but also did not make itself manifest in Needmore, Indiana, either.

Poor Hoosiers.

Better still, it would be better just to leave the mystery of how the tiny town of Gnaw Bone got its name up to the imagination. Besides, no self-respecting, down-home Hoosier will ever tell you.

Why?

There is no rhyme or reason, so it is pointless to ask.

Here is another prime example why we should never ask why.

There is no Indiana native, living or dead, who can even relate how it came to be that those living in Indiana are called Hoosiers. So, good luck trying to discover how Needmore and Gnaw Bone got their names from the indigenous people. You would have more luck finding an honest politician or moral lawyer than finding a forthcoming Hoosier willing to spill his or her guts about how Gnaw Bone and Needmore got their names.

Poor squinty-eyed Hoosiers.

Squinty-eyed or not, it was time for Mr. Local Yokel to finalize direction instructions to gullible me, Mr. Big City erudite, with the inviting face.

So with renewed enthusiasm, Mr. Local Yokel continued on with his directions. His narrative was punctuated with much arm waving and finger pointing as he patiently explained, "When you have cleared Needmore, go east for about five minutes until you see a crook in the road." (A crook in the road is idiomatic Hoosier speak for a *bend* in the road's direction and not a nefarious highway man standing in the road to facilitate criminal activity.) "And then turn off south next to the scum-covered pond that has a felled hickory tree in it."

With a long-suffering sigh, Mr. Local Yokel further instructed, "By the way, don't wear that white shirt you have on because ticks are attracted to the color white in the woods. God only knows we don't need no big-city folks coming down here and catching tick fever."

With another exasperating sigh, Mr. Local Yokel said, "We would never hear the end of it."

"Now," he said, warming up again to his subject, "keep on going down that road until you see a gravel road going off to the right, and soon enough, you'll see a small sign that identifies a trail that will take you to Plum Crick." (Again, crick is idiomatic

Hoosier speak for creek or stream and should not to be confused with a crick in the neck.) "And then you'll see the tree that has that big rock stuck up in it that people around here call Gobblers Rock."

Mr. Local Yokel scratched his ample broadside and cautioned me at once by saying, "Don't even begin to ask me why the rock in a tree has been named Gobblers Rock."

I thanked Mr. Local Yokel and made haste to get under way on my big adventure. As I exited the DQ, I looked back and couldn't help but notice Mr. Local Yokel was experiencing a coughing episode. Even though convulsive coughing is no laughing matter, his yellow teeth were fully exposed, and it seemed as if a smile was desperately trying to escape from his distorted and reddening face.

Oh, by the way, for some unknown reason, he was also holding his side while convulsing.

Poor Hoosier fellow.

I made it to the country gravel road that was meandering around in the middle of no place. *No doubt, I thought, the owls make love to the chickens in the dead of night in this place.* I replaced my white shirt with a brown one and struck off down the trail to hike to a most unusual place—a place where few have heard about and fewer still have even bothered to go.

By the way, if you have a GPS, you're in luck. Punch in the following coordinates: 39°, 12.204 north and 086°, 21.995 west. And you will end up putting a crick in your neck while looking up at the tree with a huge rock stuck in its fork, standing majestically there right alongside Plum Crick just as advertised.

If you go, take your time in getting to the GPS point because the forest is about the way it was before there was even a people called Hoosiers milling about in the area, and so there is much to see as you walk in the privileged area. Perhaps you will notice that the flora and critters haven't changed all that much since the time when the last continental glacier came to a halt on this very spot and before the stout Hoosiers began to chop down the old growth trees in a futile attempt to eke out a living in these parts.

If you would have gotten to the designated GPS coordinates a couple of years ago, you would have found that mighty eighty-foot oak tree on the banks of Plum Creek (or Plum Crick as the indigenous folk still call it), and if you looked up, you would have seen a very large brown sandstone boulder wedged in a branch fork about thirty feet up.

However, a mighty storm racked the area awhile back and felled the once mighty tree with the terrestrial interloper called Gobblers Rock still locked in its branches. The tree fell with the pictured stone still firmly wedged in its fork, and it now lies on the forest floor instead of reaching for the sky with its strange burden. Nature had finally pulled it down.

But wait. There's more. There are a number of trees that are still standing around in the same area that have big rocks in their branches. I have went to these places and seen the strange sight of boulders in the treetops with my own eyes. Along with many others, I have speculated how the heavy rocks could find themselves up in trees.

Many experts have speculated about how the rocks defied gravity and lodged themselves in the tops of trees, but in reality, no one really knows. There are two prominent theories concerning this mystery. First, some said that drunken Indiana University (IU) students put the heavy stones in the trees by some unknown means and that they did so because it seemed like the thing to do at the time with the added benefit of confounding the local Hoosier yahoos. Others said that a UFO had visited the area and put the stones up in the trees.

I personally think that the first theory is the most plausible one because I have seen the many implausible and mysterious things that drunken IU students have done in the past.

As far as the UFO theory goes, think about it. Why would a species smart enough to build spaceships that can motor about the cosmos find it necessary to go to Needmore, Indiana, in order to place heavy rocks in the tops of trees?

Would they do so to confound Hoosiers? I think not. After all, there are many lesser things that confound Hoosiers. Hoosiers are still confounded about the change to daylight saving time, so placing heavy rocks up in the trees would not seem a worthy endeavor by an advanced race.

But there is something else about those rocks in the trees.

Rocks do not belong in the top of trees.

Rocks belong on the ground with all of their brother and sister rocks.

We all know this to be true.

So it must not be just a matter of how the rock got lodged high up in the tree that is important. It must also be a matter that the tree rock is an out-of-place rock. It is this salient fact of being out of place that makes the tree rock an unusual rock.

I continued to look up at the stately tree with the extraordinary rock while contemplating the fact that the levitated rock was, indeed, an unusual out-of-place rock.

And then it struck me like a lightning bolt.

What if a person was like the rock in a tree?

Think about it.

What if some unknown force or circumstance had also situated a person into a place where normal "go along to get along" people could never occupy? Perhaps an unusual place that made the person different from his or her conventional and grounded brothers and sisters.

If that were to happen, then perhaps normal brothers and sisters might judge these out-of-place people to be unusual at best and antisocial at worst.

For example, if the tree rock were a person, the lofty place up in the tree would afford the rock-person a different perspective on things because of his or her expanded horizon. The expanded perspective would be different and unintelligent to rock comrades on the ground because of their limited perspective of the horizon at ground level.

After this realization the metaphor became real and complete.

There are indeed those among us who are just like those rocks stuck up in trees. The rocks are stuck in a place where they do not belong, and there are those of us who are also stuck in a place where we do not belong.

Some call these out-of-place people *contrarians* because they always seem out of place with their contrary opinions and counterarguments. Perhaps these people are contrarians because life's circumstances have placed them in unusual places that have afforded them different perspectives from their fellow man. And so they are always at odds with their brothers and sisters, even though they don't necessarily want to be disconnected from the rest of the "go along to get along" crowd.

Moreover, some might call these out-of-place individuals *sovereigns*[1] because they always seem out of place because of their single-minded determination to live free lives unencumbered by a necessity to "go along to get along." Perhaps these people are sovereigns because life's circumstances have also afforded them different perspectives from their fellow man. Sovereigns are

---

[1] Modern-day sovereigns are individuals who refuse to bend to man-derived and arbitrary authority. Sovereigns are individuals who believe being an individual is about as human as anyone can get. And so sovereigns believe the only legal authority they are required to follow is their own moral compass and their God (or nature if you prefer). They have the right to live as they see fit within the framework of just laws and social norms. A more historical and common name for sovereign man is a person who is a practitioner of the laissez-faire philosophy.

dedicated to the notion that living a constrained life is not living at all.

I think it would be difficult to find a distinguishing difference between a contrarian and a sovereign because both have the same inherent perceptions about freedom, fairness, and justice. It is this commonality of perception and sense that makes them seem like one and the same.

Perhaps there is a viable reason why these contrarians and sovereigns have this intrinsic characteristic that affects their ethical judgments. And further, it appears that the intrinsic characteristic has been hardwired into their genome. And further still, the intrinsic characteristic has been passed on to us all somehow.

Most people find it extraordinary that all people on this beautiful blue planet share the same concept about fairness, justice, and freedom whether they are contrarians, sovereigns, or just plain and ordinary humans of every race, color, and creed.

If you think about it, perhaps it's not all that extraordinary after all.

Consider how we all have come to be where we are today, even in modern society. Our modern society is populated by humans who have survived an unbroken chain of inherited traits from the same parents of us all who lived throughout the various epochs of human social development. The foundation for most of the inherited traits occurred during the first and most prolonged epoch, the hunter/gather society. It only requires logic and common sense to see how the notions of freedom, fairness, and justice got hardwired into mankind's genome during the hunter/gather epoch.

Consider how people lived life during the hunter/gather epoch and how they sowed the seeds that have sprouted into the concept of freedom, fairness, and justice, even in today's modern society.

Freedom

Hunters and gathers had no crops to work, no land to defend, no taxes to pay, no army to support, and no nobility to bend down to. They took from nature whatever they needed without regard, and when the opportunity presented itself, they traveled to wherever and whenever they pleased and did so without permission. Sounds like the very definition of freedom to me.

Fairness

Fairness was learned. It was born of necessity so that people could survive the hardships and reality of primitive life. It has been said that life is cruel. I don't believe that is correct. Life is fair rather than cruel because it treats all equally without regard to status or station. Some may feel this is cruel because some do not adjust to Mother Nature's laws, and so they pay a steep price for not doing so.

If a member of the hunter/gather tribe does not participate in the labor and effort to obtain food and maintain the tribe, that person would not be permitted to share in the bounty produced by the labor and efforts of others. Not participating would mean less people would have to do more in order to provide for those who did not participate. This would eventually result in an unsustainable situation that would doom all.

Furthermore, the situation would no doubt result in communal strife and unproductive activity, adding to an increasing loss of effort to obtain food and maintain the community. So began the concept of fairness. The slacker was not afforded the benefits obtained by others because it was not fair to do so. The freeloader paid a steep price for not working as hard as all others, and this person probably did not survive his or her malfeasance.

His probable death means he was not afforded the opportunity to pass on his freeloading traits to his progeny and us. Life may be considered cruel, but only because it is fair. People learned this lesson because only those who practiced fairness survived to live another day and pass on the lesson to future humans.

Justice

Justice is fairness's diplomacy. If you do not practice fairness and live within the accepted societal norms, justice would be swift and awful. Justice is only just when done equally to all who practice fairness and live within the societal norms (and all who do not).

The tale that proceeds from this preface is a story about a man who is not only a contrarian but a devoted sovereign as well.

This contrarian/sovereign person has a name.

His name is Thaddeus Jones or TJ, as he will come to be called.

Mysterious forces beyond anyone's understanding propelled Thaddeus Jones into his unusual place. TJ had a different perspective about life in general, one brought about by an expanded horizon because of his circumstances.

That is to say, TJ is a rock in a tree.

Encoded within his genes, TJ is the one who always questions why things are the way they are.

Why TJ was condemned to this contrarian/sovereign role is to ask why the big bang happened or why DNA self-assembled out of a primordial soup of muck.

The reality is that TJ was somehow chosen by the unpredictable and fickle forces of happenstance, to be the one to engage in a perpetual war against the ubiquitous forces that continually strive to remake man (who's endowed with freedom) into a malleable automaton (who's directed by the state).

Sovereign Mr. Thaddeus Jones, Esquire, will have none of it.

Oh, by the way, there are a number of real-life people who would feel rather honored to be labeled rocks in a tree, and here are just a few. There's

- Albert Einstein,
- Winston Churchill,
- Nelson Mandela,
- Martin Luther King,
- Martin Luther,
- Jesus Christ,
- Mahatma Gandhi,
- Siddhartha Gautama (Buddha),
- Kong Qiu (Confucius),
- Marcus Cicero,
- Howard Hughes,
- George Washington,
- John Locke,
- James Madison, and
- William Buckley.

And perhaps that list could even include you or me.

INTRODUCTION

When you read *Rocks in Trees*, you may notice a similarity between the stories about the mission of Don Quixote to restore chivalry and our hero's mission to advance the notion of sovereign man. The missions of our two heroes may be somewhat similar because of the idealistic hopelessness of their endeavors, but that is where the similarity ends.

Don Quixote rose to the challenge of trying to restore chivalry as society's operational paradigm, while Thaddeus Jones blusters along in a hopeless meandering journey to reestablish personal independence as modern society's operational paradigm.

In short, Don Quixote was looking backward at the time when chivalry supported feudalism during the agricultural age, while Thaddeus Jones is looking forward to a time when the sovereignty of man can support a universal commonwealth of man[2] in the fourth societal epoch, now called the information age.

Nobility's use of chivalry to support the feudal era during the agricultural age was the operational paradigm that facilitated the exchange of man's service and labor for use of the land. Adam Smith's invisible hand of the free marketplace is the operational paradigm that will facilitate the unrestricted movement of ideas, thought, and enterprise of sovereign man in exchange for peaceful use of the planet's living space during the information age without a neo-nobility's governance. (See the Afterword, Neonobilty, at the end of this story.)

In Thaddeus Jones's view, sovereign man is the only way a commonwealth of man can become a reality and thus free man once and for all from the clutches of overpowering government and its pompous intellectual minions. And once man is finally freed from the clutches of the self-appointed elite neo-nobility, the free and unrestricted movement of ideas, thought, and

---

[2] In the author's view, a commonwealth of man is the next logical step in societal evolution if man is ever to survive his use of technology to subjugate his fellow man. That is, rather than using technology to subjugate and kill people, technology should and can be used to create a commonwealth of man by making all people sovereign. The wealth that is to be made common among all sovereign people is the free exchange of ideas, thought, and enterprise that the invisible hand of the free marketplace will make available to all peoples during the information age. Unrestricted use of the Internet, the World Wide Web, and all of their refinements is the mechanism to facilitate the free exchange of ideas, thought, and enterprise. That movement can bring about the true Age of Aquarius and save us all. The Internet is also paving the way for a commonwealth of man as the printing press furthered the enlightenment of man. This idea is advanced in the book *The Sovereign Individual: How to Survive and Thrive during the Collapse of the Welfare State* by James Dale Davidson and William Rees-Mogg.

enterprise during the information age will usher in a peaceful commonwealth of man.

It's impossible to state that a commonwealth of man would be the endpoint to establish the illusive idea of utopia, which has served both as a supreme human social goal and a mechanism to subjugate idealistic but gullible people. Perhaps society would be best served by considering the concept of utopia like beauty—that is, utopia and beauty are both "in the eye of the beholder." So while utopia and beauty is only a subjective belief that isn't shared by all, a commonwealth of man can be a reality that all ethical and rational people can embrace.

At this point, we need to step back to examine man's advancement from a time when he rubbed two sticks together in order to make fire to now when he can rub two atoms together in order to free up the energy of the universe.

Most agree that man is now living in the fourth world or societal epoch. We are now transitioning from the industrial age into the new and improved informational age. The four great societal epochs include (1) hunting and gathering societies, (2) agricultural societies, (3) industrial societies, and (4) informational societies.

Interestingly, Hopi Indian history[3] also relates that man is now living in the fourth world and that the time between epochs shortens with each passing epoch (just as the time between the four societal epochs shortens with each passing epoch). Furthermore, reading the Hopi account of human history and comparing that description of man's transitioning from one epoch to another is also remarkable in that a common thread meanders throughout the Hopi account and our modern understanding of the history of mankind. To date, human societies have been unable to contain

---

3   From the book *The History of the Hopi from Their Origins in Lemuria* by Oswald White Bear Fredericks and Keith Khriste King.

the destructive impulses that make us all unique, and that uniqueness has to do with the very human condition called ego.

Ego is the essence of man and gives rise to the notion of sovereign man.

Ego is what makes us human, and it is also what drives us to battle our fellow man for dominance so that we can survive and continuously advance. This is why both accounts of mankind's history are really a distressing and common story about the struggle of mankind to keep from destroying one another while *progressing* to a new and better societal world.

Well, here is another distressing thought. We have finally managed to progress to the point where the real possibility exists that modern technology will enable someone's ego to finally trump reason and completely destroy all of mankind once and for all time.

And so all of the man's governing schemes and philosophies have all tried to deal with the dichotomy of ego and the necessity of common preservation while trying to continuously advance to a new and better society. However, nothing to date has really advanced us to that desired—and subjective—utopia that is always just beyond the reach of man's ego.

To further understand the ego, modern man has defined the ego as an –ism, and that normative egoism has two positions, namely rational egoism and ethical egoism. You may distinguish between the two in the following way: Rational egoism argues that acting only in one's self-interest will benefit all (raising tides lifting all boats, trickle-down economics, etc.). However, ethical egoism argues that acting for the benefit of all will be in one's self-interest (no man is an island, etc.).

Well, if you can agree with the distinction between egos, the dichotomy of the ego that strives to advance mankind without destroying one another is plainly there for all to contemplate.

Furthermore, in the political realm, you can easily make an assertion that rational egoism really describes the modern conservative political position quite well while ethical egoism most assuredly describes the modern socialist political position.

The story of *Rocks in Trees* posits the notion that we can finally manage the dichotomy of ego-directed conflict and cooperation by supporting the position that the invisible hand of the free marketplace will support the argument for rational egoism, thus enabling a commonwealth of man. And a commonwealth of man will then support the argument for ethical egoism. Thus, a commonwealth of man can be the bridge to converge and connect the two conflicting ego forces into a balanced force for a common cause.

So perhaps, the reality of a commonwealth of man can finally provide the means to reconcile rational egoism with ethical egoism into a workable way to bring about modern societal enlightenment, and with it, a world made peaceful and graceful for all people.

And just maybe, the reality of a commonwealth of man could only be made possible by the sovereignty of man that requires a *Rock in Tree* to facilitate.

This could be what the sunshine boys call a win-win situation.

PROLOGUE

Five trillion, twenty-two billion, one hundred and eighty-seven million, five hundred thousand (5,022,187,500,000) and some odd days ago, the eggheads tell us our universe *sprung* into existence as a result of a resounding and really big bang.

One trillion, six hundred and fifty-eight billion, two hundred and thirty-five million (1,658,235,000,000) and some odd days ago, the eggheads tell us our planet coalesced out of a cosmic junk pile and began to orbit a benevolent star called the Sun. The orbiting collection of rocks and other cosmic debris would eventually be called Earth (Gaea) by the sentient life that would eventually come to live there.

One trillion and some odd days ago, the eggheads also tell us the sentient life referenced previously had its origins as a form of extremely primitive life. The eggheads further tell us that the initial fortuitous self-origination event of primitive life would eventually give rise to the previously mentioned sentient life because of a Charles Darwin-inspired theory called evolution.

The eggheads also tell us that evolution was indeed responsible for advancing the life that *sprung* forth from the ooze and muck of a nightmare Earth environment and evolving into the beautiful people who now enrich our daily lives on network TV, in Hollywood movies, and in the well of the US Congress.

However, the eggheads have never bothered to explain how it happened that life managed to self-originate in such an inspired and intellectual manner that somehow included the operational paradigm of evolution to constantly and perpetually advance life into more and more complexity. The laws of physics prohibit a system (such as life) from perpetually increasing in complexity and yet life does it. And it does so by using physics in an intellectual, not fundamental, manner. If indeed the operational paradigm of evolution works in the way the theory posits, evolution itself must also be a random, self-originating fortuitous design of the very life that is indigenous to the basic wonder of life. So if life somehow managed to self-originate, it could only do so with the theory of evolution firmly embodied within the design of its basic life system. Then the resultant life that we know of today would be capable of enduring while forever increasing in complexity as long as life itself existed.[4]

That sure is a lot of random, fortuitous, and self-originating serial events happening to make all of these things work out.

You know, another one of those inexplicable chicken and egg things.

Us pedestrians can only cogitate about these kinds of egghead theories that feeds a gnawing discontent with the Holier-Than-Thou scientific and egg head community that insist that only they know the truth, the whole truth, and nothing but the truth.

One thing we know for sure is this: Members of the US Congress and bankers are forever indebted to the wonderful theory of evolution for their positions in the human pecking order while also enjoying their lofty positions in the food chain.

---

[4] Self-originate, beginning with, or springing from one's self.
Originate, **the point at which something comes into existence or from which it derives or is derived.**

We can stew forever about how and why the three really important things happened that the Eggheads tell us *sprung forth* without warning or explanation (the creation of the universe, planet Earth coalescing into a rotating sphere with gobs of water and life-sustaining environments, and finally, life itself sparking into existence from the ooze and muck of inanimate matter on Mother Earth).

Suffice to say, these three things did happen. As everyone knows, even know-it-all eggheads, really big things always happen in threes. That's about as scientific as any of us pedestrians can possible be about these three important matters.

No one living today can tell us how it came to be that the eggheads became so much smarter than the rest of us. It must be another of those fortuitous things that just happens, but lucky for us pedestrians, it happened because the eggheads are here today to impart all of the previously mentioned important knowledge to the rest of us. And we are much blessed and are able to live our lives to the fullest extent possible because of all of this imparted knowledge.

Well, most of us do so.

Ten thousand, nine hundred and fifty-seven (10,957) and some odd days ago on Mother Earth, a modern human man and woman were having casual sex in a spacious Chevy SUV. As a result of their exuberance and libertine attitude, they inadvertently created a male child. The accidental child would eventually grow into a man, and that man would be called Thaddeus Jones or TJ to his acquaintances. But sadly, he would have only one real friend, but more about that later.

To say that Thaddeus Jones was an important and incredibly significant part of the creation of the universe, that is, the planet Earth coalescing into a rotating sphere with gobs of water and life-sustaining environments and the miracle of life sparking itself into existence from the ooze and muck of inanimate matter on Mother Earth would be an understatement of such grand proportions that it could contract the whole of the known universe down to a single troupe of dancing angels on a pinhead. You know, sort of like the entire universe contracting down to an infinitesimal singularity and then dancing outward to a complex big bang majestic opera.

That is, even though TJ came about due to a spontaneous event, his beginning could have only happened because of the really big three spontaneous events that created all that we know, Nevertheless, TJ did spring into being without warning or explanation just like the universe, Mother Earth, and magnificent life itself, and the rest of the civilized world will just have to learn how to deal with the reality of it all.

That is to say, TJ was never destined to be in any way shape or form an important egghead. He instead would leave his mark upon his fellow man as a contrarian and one who could never understand why his fellow men did what they do. Regrettably, TJ would never quite fit in with the rest of modern civil humanity. In today's vernacular, Thaddeus Jones is a postmodern man with the self-assuring benefit of not caring one wit about what postmodern even means.

That is to say, Thaddeus Jones was also a sovereign man.

Yes, it's sad but true. TJ will be a man buoyed by an unbounded sense of righteousness made even more dangerous by being armed with a bountiful measure of misdirected wit. That is to say, TJ's intellectual quiver had a full complement of pointy arrows to launch at friend and foe alike, but his intellectual fusillade always seemed to miss the mark of anything approaching relevance to his working-day fellow man.

Nevertheless, TJ's intellectual arsenal was enabled somehow, and it would be used again and again with forceful determination and a dogged mind-set.

This single-minded characteristic would not endear him to his fellow man or more importantly, to the state-appointed masters of government control.

Poor fellow.

Perhaps this is what can happen when a crapshoot of embracing chromosomes mix up a new batch of DNA by somehow picking and choosing genes inherited from in-heat and nonchalant parents. All in all, a chromosome crapshoot big bang event every bit as mysterious as the big bang event that brought forth the universe and the Supreme Court of the United States.

However, this particular mysterious biological big bang event brought forth a living, breathing Thaddeus Jones, which in a marvelous sense is just as important and relevant as the big bang that brought forth our physical universe. And further, it is just as marvelous as the original biological event that brought forth the genesis of self-originating life from the ooze and muck of primal Mother Earth.

Perhaps we have somehow achieved symmetry here. The same biological big bang event that brought forth Thaddeus Jones from the ooze and muck of modern humans on the backseat of a Chevy SUV is in reality a continuation of the same biological big bang event that brought forth the genesis of self-originating life from the ooze and muck of primal Mother Earth.

Who knew?

CHAPTER 1

And Along Came TJ

Thaddeus Jones came into the cold reality of life headfirst, screaming his tiny lungs out. A straining and sweating female, eager to rid herself of the burden acquired as a result of a night of sweet abandon and exciting promiscuity, forcibly expelled TJ from his privileged existence on one nondescript April evening.

With a final exhausted grunt, the female, reduced to primal obligations, dislodged the little male from her expanded self, and she did so with very little decorum and with much relief.

Thaddeus Jones (TJ) was delivered alive and kicking without knowing how he came to be or why he had been cast out from his warm and benevolent domicile. TJ was too young and ignorant to have knowledge about what had caused his spirit to be hatched out in the first place.

Was it a chance alignment of the stars that sparked TJ into existence from a crapshoot of philandering sperm and opportunistic egg?

Not likely.

The stars are really not responsible for ensuring planet Earth is continuously and fully populated with bipedal and sexually active humans. Somehow, an exquisite biological program of action has been encoded into the human genome, and that program of action short-circuits all rational thought whenever an opportunity presents itself to make more humans.

And so, apparently, opportunities to make more humans arise all the time here on Mother Earth (Gaia). There seems to be an unlimited supply of new humans wandering about and voting every day. So in no way is a chance alignment of stars responsible for this remarkable creative situation. Only a robust and magnificent biological program could be responsible for making all of the new humans who are busting the limited seams of Mother Earth's skirt.

The incalculable numbers of existing and new humans are not only voting but also eating everything in sight while extracting treasure from the bosom of Mother Earth to suit their private and public fancy. This is apparently what happens when you have a vigorous biological program in an inviting and benign environment.

Of course, this biological program has been aided and abetted throughout time by an unlimited supply of testosterone-saturated sperm donors and an equal supply of estrogen-gilded sperm recipients who together execute the biological program with unerring perfection. However, the program is made easier when the sperm recipient has been made even more receptive by the liberal use of caution-inhibiting alcohol.

All testosterone-driven sperm donors instinctually know about the rewarding effects of alcohol on estrogen-motivated sperm recipients. Perhaps this embedded knowledge concerning the marvelous properties of alcohol is an intrinsic part of the inexplicable biological program to promulgate the human species. One thing, however, is patently obvious. The functional biological program to perpetuate human existence is foolproof in every sense of the word.

Moreover, who among us could write such an elegant program anyway? Modern eggheads? I think not. Modern eggheads first looked at a rendering of the elegant DNA in the human genome and declared, "Most of the DNA in the human genome is junk DNA." That's right. The same eggheads that now tell us CO_2 is a pollutant are part and parcel of the same science fraternity that told us that the DNA responsible for all life on Mother Earth is mostly junk.

You know, the CO_2 that is the lifeblood of all things green and the essential by-product of all animal life has been declared a poison. Yes, that's right. These are the same eggheads armed with only the arrogance of a little knowledge (and a lot of arrogant assurance) who tell us dumb-butt pedestrians the exquisitely designed human DNA is mostly junk.

Well nevertheless, on a warm and friendly night in July, when the twinkling unaligned stars could care less, the junk DNA assisted the primal sexual urges that executed the foolproof biological program on the rear seat of a Chevy SUV, and TJ was conceived. And thus, TJ was inadvertently sparked into existence and made a part of the dynamic human gene pool.

Before TJ was cast out kicking and screaming, one can only speculate how the sperm donor and sperm recipient related to each other as the female womb and bosom began their expansion to larger and larger dimensions, making their secret night of sexual exhilaration public fodder for easy and juicy gossip.

As if anyone really cared what Mr. Sperm Donor and Miss Sperm Recipient had occasion to do in the backseat of a Chevy SUV. Most gossipers only feel fortunate they have the opportunity to feel superior by noting their fellow man's egalitarian misfortunes. But nevertheless, regardless what the chattering yeomen of gossip think or say, most fraternal sperm donors can certainly relate to the gut-wrenching Sunday morning phone call that almost always goes something like this. "Hey, dipshit, I'm pregnant."

Most sister sperm recipients can certainly relate to the inevitable reply from the clueless dipshits that likely goes something like this. "Are you sure? Why are you telling me?"

And now we must ask, "Is this a great biological program or what?"

And thus begins the real-life soap opera that countless other sperm donors and sperm recipients have found themselves acting in as the featured characters in an opus as old as life itself. It must be hard to celebrate the miracle of life when the duty dipshit can only think, *How am I going to support this little fucker for the next twenty some odd years? I was destined to sail all of the south sea islands and make love to all of the exotic and uninhibited women I chanced to meet. Now instead I'll have to get a dumb-ass job and sail a company desk while some Captain Numb Nuts keeps yelling at me to get on the ball.*

It must be even more difficult for the willing sperm recipient to adjust to the reality that soon a little ball-hanger will now be sucking on her beautiful breasts until they sag into milk jugs. The days when her stunning figure and proud breasts could inspire beautiful songs, lovely poems, and hunky men fighting over the privilege to get next to her will now be gone.

And now the lovely pregnant female who wanted to be the fist-liberated woman of her clan to march to her own drum and show the world some new and different moves will have to instead exercise the same old moves that all of the other pedestrian women in the world have had to execute since evolution invented the sex drive.

So instead of becoming an inspirational role model for all wannabe liberated women, she is now faced with the certainty of constant care for a growing and demanding tiny human who cares little that she can no longer march to the drumbeat of carefree and independent living.

Yes, that's right, Virginia. Santa Claus knocked you up instead of bringing you the liberated and exciting life you dreamed of.

Well, you can plainly see that the conceivers of one Thaddeus Jones may have conceived the little dude, but they will never be in serious contention for the Dr. Benjamin McLane Spock Loving Family Award. Nevertheless, the sperm donor and sperm recipient managed to reconcile themselves to the fact they are now single parents responsible for the care, feeding, education, and support of one brand-new human boy.

Ah yes, the little boy would eventually grow into an adult and pose this astute question to an indifferent world, "Why are men of small stature more susceptible to becoming mean pricks rather than becoming nice guys like me?"

Who among us really knows the answer to such society-shaking questions? However, here is what we do know. Little TJ was conceived as a result of primal sexual urges given passage by an aggressive sperm donor and an alcohol-fueled compliant sperm recipient on a dark, warm, and friendly night in July. Perhaps our inquiring minds can conjure up a connection between the magical mixing of disparate chromosomes and the obligatory rearing by apathetic parents as somehow responsible for the eventual adult who would find it necessary to ask such a question.

If only people were smart enough, they could make the connections between circumstances, cause, and effect and then determine what would happen in the future as a result of those connections and circumstances. Perhaps the passionate backseat event, if it was indeed a prescient moment that gave rise to TJ, could indeed predict the future of one little TJ.

There are lots of people who think they are smart enough to make knowledgeable predictions like this, and they do it each and every day. And they make these predictions to anyone they can corral long enough to demonstrate their wisdom in these matters.

Wow, those people must be a lot smarter than most of us.

If TJ's conception was indeed a prescient moment, then there must be many more such prescient occasions that really smart and enlightened people can recognize as transformative events.

So we would be remiss if we didn't explore the possibility of other prescient moments, such as the election of a president. Some really astute and enlightened people claim to know what the future will bring upon electing any president. Not only that, there are a number of enlightened and smart people who never hesitate to impart their superior knowledge about what the future will bring as a result of any number of prescient moments, including

- the direction and magnitude of future divine providence,
- the magnitude and direction of impending forces of nature,
- the Zodiac alignment with the stars,
- the fundamental transformation of an entire country,
- when hope and change will replace gloom and doom,
- when gloom and doom will replace hope and change,
- the number of Beatles albums that will be sold,
- the possibility that patriotic Democrats or Republicans will be elected,
- the direction and magnitude of the DOW Jones industrial average,
- the rise and fall of home mortgage rates,
- the rise and fall of women's skirts,
- the future sales of Viagra,
- when the fish will bite,
- when your hair will turn gray,
- when the first snow will fall,

Rocks in Trees

- when your Chevy heap finally will blow,
- when your belly size finally will exceed the magnitude of your libido,
- when your children will start/stop asking you for advice,
- when the dollar will be equal to a 1920 penny,
- when inflation will stop,
- when Christianity will become relevant again,
- when everyone will become as smart as you,
- when the Colts will win another Super Bowl,
- When your Mother stops trying to feed you,
- when your Father will think you really do know the difference between shit and Shinola,
- the price of gasoline tomorrow,
- when certain men will decide to do a comb-over,
- when women will stop asking if their butts are getting bigger,
- when stockbrokers will become honest,
- when preachers will live like they tell us to live,
- when spending will not exceed income,
- when people will know the difference between a politician and a used car salesman,
- when a professional golfer will make less money than the president,
- when the South will rise again,
- When progressives will stop telling everyone else how to live,
- when conservatives will finally become as smart as progressives,
- when we will never trust poor lawyers,
- when we will never trust rich lawyer, and
- when we will never trust lawyers in general.

7

Really smart people could know all of these future things if only they were astute enough to divine the proper connections between seemly unrelated circumstances of prescient moments, such as when newbie TJ was conceived and joined the collective human gene pool and perhaps when the president was elected and was transmuted into the smartest person alive on planet Earth.

But then again, the truth may well be that the enthusiastic moment in the backseat of that Chevy SUV is only one of an infinite number of ongoing biological moments that were somehow programmed in the human genome and was not an ordained prescient event after all.

That is to say, the sperm donor and sperm recipient were only doing what comes naturally, and as such, they can no more determine how little TJ will turn out as an adult any more than people can foretell the outcome of any important event. It's possible we couldn't divine these things even if we were the smartest people in the entire universe and Canada.

However, here is what people do know. Little TJ was forcibly expelled on an April evening. He came from a warm and gracious natal sanctuary, and he was brought into the brightly lit and shockingly cold, environs of a industrial-size, moneymaking health care machine that we call a modern hospital complex.

TJ was not happy.

His raucous unhappiness was projected upon the duty hospital troupe. They responded to his primitive lament with practiced and professional indifference. To compound the injustice, a smack on the butt was administered with no love at all, and plastic things were shoved up his nose, mouth, and other unmentionable places with cool efficiency by mask-covered health automatons who were just doing their jobs.

Just like the beginning of the universe and the genesis of life on Mother Earth, all of these things happened without explanation or warning to the brand-new miracle of life.

The warm and gracious sanctuary from which TJ was expelled had been, prior to his expulsion, his very own privileged and personal domicile that had provided for all of his wants and needs. And now through no fault of his own, he had been forcibly removed from his very own personal utopia like one would be cast out as an unwelcome interloper.

So in response to his being cast out, the squirming little wonder was protesting his new circumstances in the only manner available to him. He was crying as hard and as loud as he possibly could.

If only TJ could have been capable of understanding words, he would have heard the uniformed health professional say, "There, there, little fellow, stop your crying now. We are doing this for your own good."

As God is our witness, many others of our kind do have a basic understanding of words and their meaning, and when we hear words like those the health automaton uttered to little TJ, we, too, can become terrified out of our wits.

For example, a smug and confident government automaton could arrive one day on your doorstep. The government automaton wearing a dark suit proclaiming his ubiquitous jurisdiction, could announce with a knowing smile and arrogant demeanor, "Hello there, I'm from the government, and I'm here to help you."

Any person with one lick of sense will fall into an immediate funk upon hearing those words, and the funk will prevail until the government help finally goes away—that is, if it ever does.

The brand-new TJ cannot yet understand the soothing words of his attendants, and so he keeps on protesting anyway because he was not where he wanted to be. In a curious twist, helpless adults are much like helpless TJ because we, too, hear the insidious words of government help and protest loudly. We know only too well that we will be forced into an uncomfortable position not of our choosing.

Of course, little TJ could not have known his conception on the backseat of a Chevy SUV by an enthusiastic sperm donor and a willing sperm recipient was the act that would eventually lead to his summary discharge from utopia. TJ only sensed that he did not want to be where he was now and that he was not at all happy about the circumstance of his existence.

This sense of being out of place and the resulting unhappiness would continue to blossom unabated into his adulthood and have many consequences for TJ and us all. These many consequences would come to guide TJ's life like a category-five hurricane driving a sailing vessel into harm's way.

Poor fellow.

TJ did not have a choice about how he came to be or how he obtained his characteristics from his parents. Chance alone mysteriously ordained TJ to be like a rock in a tree.

Poor fellow.

Somehow, TJ's chromosomes would build a mind and persona that could only find relevance when he could challenge and annoy law-abiding citizens by always going against the arrow, marching away from the pointing finger, and bravely always going in the out door.

Perhaps there is something to this prescient business after all.

CHAPTER 2

The A Precedes the B Because

The accidental parents of little TJ struggled to be responsible guardians without the benefit of being married and all of that old-fashioned stuff. Actually, they also suffered from not being a nuclear family while attending to their parental duties. They both admitted, during an unguarded moment, somehow enabled by chugging down some McDonald's chemistry-inspired food and sharing a Hap-Hap-Happy Meal with little TJ.

TJ's dad complained, "It's tough trying to be a real mom and dad on a part-time basis and sharing parenting responsibilities during all of the individual comings and goings because of the separate demands of job, friends, and family."

It's a sign of the times that these accidental parents were not even an exception in the parenting world. The situation they found themselves in is, in fact, fast becoming the new normal in the wired-up, hooked-up, 4G, new and improved, politically correct United States of America.

While the responsible parents of little TJ didn't actually subscribe to the Hillary Clinton–celebrated utopian notion that it takes a village to raise a child, they nevertheless eagerly accepted all the help they could get, whether it came from the government, friends, family, or even a the New Harmony (Indiana) self-sustaining utopian village.

Because why not?

That is, if help is available, why not accept it?

Why not use it?

Perhaps the "why not" should be cause to examine the reality that the urgent road of expediency is not necessarily the path you would normally choose to follow. Experience has shown that expedient *help* always comes with strings attached.

The problem being, of course, is that expediency is the first and foremost excuse for not doing the hard and correct thing. That is, expediency, expediency, hurry me down to calamity.

And once you are on the easy freeway of expediency, U-turns are rarely permitted and off-ramps are few and far between.

TJ's parents even flirted with the idea of getting married and cohabitating in an open marriage to make parenting more manageable and to reduce the cost of their new obligations. However, upon further review, the modern parents of one Thaddeus Jones could not bring themselves to deliberately contemplate such a new and complicated approach to modern living.

TJ's parents were traveling down an unmarked path while struggling to do the right thing by their new obligation. Doing the right thing that was aided and abetted by what their old-fashioned Mamas and Papas drummed into them long ago about the necessity of moral living being the only viable recipe for life, liberty, and the pursuit of happiness. And cohabitating in an open marriage did not seem to satisfy the Mom and Pop defined moral living.

Regardless, trying to do the right thing is still far better than what lots of folks actually do nowadays.

Mr. Steven Levitt of *Freakonomics* fame once opined, "Morality is how people believe people should live. Economics is how people actually live."

Perhaps every once in a while, people take the more direct and difficult straight road of morality rather than traveling the meandering freeway of expediency. One can only speculate why some would take such moralistic approach to modern life and living.

Well, just maybe some people like Mom and Pop Jones take the straight and narrow way because in reality, it's easier to follow a moral compass to get to a known destination than dealing with the continuous stress of not knowing where the freeway of expediency will eventually lead. Without a moral compass to guide one on the straight and narrow, following the meandering freeway of expediency will always lead to an ambiguous destination.

Kudos to the full-time parents, Mom and Pop Jones, because TJ's new age parents are trying to do what's best with heaping helpings of old-fashioned morality. So with an unexpected realization that they had come to respect and depend on each other, they decided on an old-fashioned marriage after all.

Perhaps in pulpy romance novels, love comes about in a mighty rush, complete with sweating embraces and puppy-dog longing. Who can resist the sexual exuberance of a man and woman glistening from being awash in sex glow while the perfume of lovemaking makes an intoxicating and indelible memory that forever satisfies the visceral imperative that rules us all?

If only this delicious surrender to archaic sexual urges could last forever.

But of course, it doesn't.

That feeling lasting forever would be a fantasy.

However, in real life, lasting love usually takes time to make itself manifest. Things like respect, honor, devotion, and duty are just some of the basic ingredients that require time to earn and appreciate. These mundane things are the elements that can lead to real and lasting love.

And when the basic ingredients have enough time to mix and the people have the patience to stir them together well, it's possible that life's oven can bake up the elegant entrée we call love. Mom and Pop Jones stirred up all of these life ingredients because of the adult decision they made to be responsible and loving parents of one Thaddeus Jones. So Mom and Pop Jones found love the old-fashioned way, which led to yet another adult decision. They decided to stand before Parson Brown, God, and the community at large to publicly vow to love, honor, and cherish each other for as long as they both lived.

Yep, they got married.

You know what?

It really is a great biological program.

Careful observers have said that parents often grow up more during the process of trying to feed, instruct, and nurture their children into becoming responsible adults. This being the case, perhaps being a responsible and successful parent should be a determining factor when voting for our political leaders. In other words, perhaps you should only vote for a candidate that has demonstrated the ability to raise a family and be a responsible adult. As a practical matter, shouldn't a demonstrated success in raising children into responsible adults be a prime factor in determining an ability to lead and be a responsible and honest politician.

Oh, my God, did we just use utter the ultimate oxymoron, "responsible and honest politician?"

Perhaps being a successful and responsible parent demonstrates the would-be leader has the necessary chops to deal with all of the demands of the childlike body politic.

If that were to happen, then maybe a "responsible and honest politician" would no longer be an oxymoron.

Well, Mom and Pop Jones were not aspiring to be politicians, but indeed, they were fast growing up as adults as they struggled with their duties to nurture their progeny into responsible adulthood. Learning how to deal with the foot-stomping tantrums of a little TJ was just one factor in the learning adventure.

There were many more learning experiences too. TJ had quickly acquired a mind of his own. It also took a lot of growing up to face down a determined little boy in such a way so that they could positively reinforce the values Mom and Pop Jones were trying to instill into the little hellion.

TJ was patiently being forced to come to grips with the notion that his mom and pop were in a unique position to instill learning as part of his growing up. His budding little mind would soon come to a realization that family etiquette would be enforced by every means available to parents. Family etiquette would require TJ learn how to deal with other people in a social environment if he was ever going to experience a measure of tranquility during his growing years.

Family etiquette and instructions on morality may have helped guide Mom and Pop Jones in doing the right thing for their little child, but TJ was still not one to suffer instructions lightly, parental or otherwise.

And so TJ would soon be just another student in PS609 after spending a tumultuous year questioning everyone and everything in Loving Care kindergarten as well as the family nest.

Mom and Pop Jones enrolled their little pain in the ass in grade school, and the little bugger was assigned—by unknown and unknowing powers—to PS609.

Say hello to one Miss Samantha Carmichael, an enthusiastic fifth-grade teacher at good old PS609.

Sam had graduated from university with a major in education. Sam was not a classic and stunning beauty like Lauren Bacall but rather more of a *Gilligan's Island* Mary Ann. Being a Mary Ann type is not in any way a negative comment about the physical appearance and charm of Samantha Carmichael.

When confronted with a choice between Mary Ann and Ginger of *Gilligan's Island* fame, men overwhelming choose Mary Ann every time. So not being a classical beauty like Lauren Bacall is in many ways much more desirable than one would expect.

Not only did Samantha Carmichael's appearance find wide and pleasing acceptance, but Sam was also a lady most people enjoy being around. Sam's personality was every bit as accommodating as her Mary Ann looks. All in all, these personal qualities made her chosen occupation as an elementary teacher a very rewarding endeavor.

Who among us was not fortunate enough to have such special elementary teachers, people we still fondly remember after so much time and experience. Well, Samantha Carmichael was just such a special person, and she had become accustomed to having dewy-eyed teenybopper boys contesting for her approval at every turn.

Little boys dreamed that their demanding mothers could somehow be just as nice as Samantha. Most little boys just wanted to get very close to Miss Carmichael without knowing the reason why they yearned to do so. They did this even at their very early age of sexual awareness, not knowing they would continue to do this even when they were no longer little boys. Indeed, some have speculated that little boys never grow up because they still behave as little boys when sex gets mixed up with complex human emotions.

But we digress.

Hey, we didn't write the human male biological program, so don't yell at the observers.

Little girls so adored Miss Carmichael that they tried to mimic her fashion, coiffure, and style, much to the bewilderment of their doting mothers desperately hoping that little Sally would copy them instead of some young role model operating without the handicap of giving birth and being a real demanding mommy. The little girl's fathers enthusiastically approved of their darling little girl's fascination with the comely Samantha. The little girl's adoration afforded the daddy the opportunity to get closer to Sam, all within accepted social norms. Accepted social norms notwithstanding, getting close to Miss Carmichael was not necessarily well received by the long-suffering moms accustomed to wayward attention by the dads.

The very same doting mommy, who heaped love and attention upon little Sally could also find benign ways to vent displeasure about the daddy's excited response to Miss Sam in a visceral way that always worked well. Mommy darlings almost always choose to vent their displeasure by not being so accommodating during the ritual time in the boudoir arena.

And it was so easy to do.

Right mommies?

Of course, the ritual boudoir activity always occurred after the evening TV newscast of murder, rape, home invasion, car accidents, fires, avalanches, hurricanes, blizzards, car chases, and avarice of every description ad infinitum. The evening newscast always had the ability to cast a pall over the ritual time in the boudoir arena with the same effectiveness as a headache or feinted physical exhaustion. Of course, the Madame of the house was well aware of the ability of the evening newscast to cool ritual ardor, and she accepted the situation as a great cover for her actions— or lack thereof—during her retaliation for a perceived wrongful relationship.

Or even because she was simply "not in the mood."

Nevertheless, Miss Carmichael soldiered on in her chosen profession in spite of the childish behavior of adults and adoring boys, large and small. She did this in spite of administrative functionaries issuing stupid and insulting orders to her and her fellow teachers. She marched on in spite of union hacks trying to turn her scared profession into a job. She steadfastly taught in spite of parents who could care less if their children became educated or not. She did this because Miss Carmichael loved teaching, and she loved teaching because she found a great deal of satisfaction in trying to shape new minds so that they accepted and appreciated the more noble side of human existence.

Thank God for the Miss Carmichaels among us.

And then one day, it happened.

Little Thaddeus Jones raised his hand in class while Miss Carmichael was teaching them about the importance of verbs, nouns, adjectives, and the like. Miss Carmichael stopped her lecture to the squirming mass of neophyte adults and recognized the little hand that was attached to one Thaddeus Jones. With his young brain firing on all cylinders, TJ demanded to know why the *a* preceded the *b* in the alphabet.

Well, it was very difficult to bring something new and demanding to the teaching table of Miss Carmichael, but TJ had done just that. The demanding little bugger momentarily stopped Miss Carmichael in her teaching tracks. She looked confused, which caused a sudden hush in the normally squirming and noisy dudes and dudettes. The children instinctually recognized something different was happening in their small sphere because Miss Carmichael suddenly looked unsure of herself in the fact of this alphabet question.

Miss Carmichael was never unsure of her abilities in the teaching discipline. She knew the answer to every question in the universe that sixth grade children could ever be expected to ask.

And yet Miss Carmichael looked puzzled and befuddled about a seemingly innocent question by a sixth grader with a strange and unnerving sparkle in his eyes.

No one had ever asked the question before—sixth grader, adult, idiot, professor, TV talking head, or alien from the Sirius star system. As the hushed children watched intently, Miss Carmichael's brain was running on overdrive, trying to remember studies concerning the English alphabet while organizing her thoughts to formulate an answer that a sixth grader could understand. She realized that something else was at stake here. If she wanted the rest of the children to continue to respect her as an all-knowing teacher, she needed an answer. If the children began to believe that Miss Carmichael did not know the answer to a simple question concerning the alphabet, how could they fully and readily accept her teachings about more complex things?

You know, things like why girls are prettier than boys.

How wonderful it is that things can get so complicated so easily. And so she began as all wise teachers and tenured politicians do. She asked a question in return in order to stall and compose herself and think about a suitable answer.

The enraptured children quickly turned to Miss Carmichael as she asked, "Thaddeus, why are you asking the question concerning the position of the letters *a* and *b* in the alphabet?"

The children, now held captive by the developing saga, just as quickly turned to TJ to hear his answer. "Miss Carmichael," he began in the squeaky voice that youth had imposed upon him, "on whose authority was the *a* placed before the *b* in the alphabet, and why was it done that way?"

With sparkling and glowing eyes, TJ further asked, "Why isn't the *b* placed before the *a* in the alphabet?"

The children thought the question by TJ was righteous and quickly turned to Miss Carmichael in order to see if she had the chops to answer the questions.

Again, Miss Carmichael asked a question in return so that she might get a better understanding of what was bugging Thaddeus about the positions of the letters in the alphabet. Most children had questions on the meaning and usage of the English letters, but no one had ever questioned the position of the letters within the accepted alphabet.

So she asked, "Why is it important to you to know how the letters of the alphabet got their positions?"

"Well," said our rock in a tree, "just because you say the alphabet starts with the letter *a* doesn't explain why we must believe you that the *a* must start the alphabet. There must be a good reason why the *a* is first, and I want to know why it is that way."

The children were absolutely and profoundly impressed that one of their snot-nose peers could put their esteemed teacher on the spot with such an innocent question.

Miss Carmichael's knees went weak with the realization that, indeed, her position as an honored teacher was at stake here, and all because this junior contrarian had the audacity to ask such an unconventional question.

Miss Carmichael tried her best not to sound patronizing when she began to answer TJ's question. She began by saying, "Thaddeus, sometimes how and why things have come to be, such as the current English alphabet, is not as important as the fact that some things are what people have come to accept. And because we all have accepted the usage, we all have the basis for understanding. There are many other alphabets in use throughout the world today. And they all have a starting letter or symbol, and they all have an ending letter or symbol. It never really occurs to most people that they should question which letter or symbol should come first because it's not as important as the alphabet itself. That is why teachers don't teach why the *a* got its first position. Do you understand what I am saying?"

TJ leaped at the teaching contradiction and hastily replied, "So you are saying we should not question the how and why of things because they have always been the way they are, and so that is why you teach the way that you do."

By now most of the children were totally lost in the argument, but they realized Thaddeus Jones was very different than the rest of them because he was having a real discussion with the teacher rather than just listening to the teacher.

Miss Carmichael was somewhat trapped by TJ's reply because teachers are instructed to teach that we should not accept convention as fact until it is proven, which is the holy grail of teaching. Teachers didn't want to indoctrinate.

Miss Carmichael recanted, "Well, I didn't mean to suggest you should not question how things are, but I was trying to explain that some things don't need to be fully known to be useful to one's education."

"However," Miss Carmichael continued, "I hope you can understand what I am about to relate to you about our English alphabet because this is only taught to language students at a very high level of understanding. But here goes. The alphabet we use today had it beginning long, long ago as a means to represent language by the use of letters. Many different peoples had a hand in developing the alphabet we use today, and it is generally called the Semitic script. But in truth, the first true alphabet was an alphabet developed by the ancient Greek people. It so happens that the word *alpha* means the *beginning* in Greek, and because the word alpha starts with the letter *a*, the letter *a* naturally became the first letter in our alphabet, which has been passed down to us."

The entire classroom was mesmerized by Miss Carmichael's explanation, even though they had no idea what she was talking about. What they did understand, however, was one Thaddeus Jones, their classmate, was so different than themselves that they all looked at him as though he was an alien from the Sirius star system that had somehow landed in their classroom. Their astonishment only increased when TJ considered Miss Carmichael's explanation, and after a long and thoughtful moment, he declared, "Oh, okay. I now understand. Thank you, Miss Carmichael."

The children in Miss Carmichael's class were abuzz with excitement as they replayed among themselves what had just happened in their classroom. They could not wait to get home so that they could relate every delicious detail to their parents and anyone with ears.

However, Miss Carmichael was not all that excited about what had happened because she was rather taken aback by the sudden acquiescence by Thaddeus to her explanation. What a strange and different little fellow TJ was, and she speculated about how life would be for TJ as adulthood caught up with him.

Miss Carmichael could hardly wait for lunchtime so that she could relate to her teaching peers what had happened in her classroom because of the strange little dude named Thaddeus Jones.

After Miss Carmichael had faithfully relayed what had happened, her teaching peers made careful note of TJ, who was now a marked student. Each and every one of Miss Carmichael's teaching peers shuddered at the thought of having to deal with the peculiar little shit, Thaddeus Jones, in their very own classroom.

Even at his young age, Thaddeus Jones usually caused people like grade school teachers to avoid personal encounters regardless of the circumstances, and so friends were hard to come by. TJ was not happy about his lack of personal charisma with people, but he was beginning to understand he was different. He and the rest of the world would just have to learn how to deal with their differences.

Perhaps, he mused, he was one of the few out of a multitude of people who had a mission in life. He relished the thought, and the more he thought about it, the more liked the idea of having a mission. He liked the idea because even as a neophyte human male, he was aware that most people just meandered through life like helpless flotsam driven by societal currents and waves.

And by some unknown force of nature, he had a mission.

So he really had to be different if he had a mission when most others had none. TJ continued to think about this and decided that if he indeed had a mission, that mission would surely be to question every law, rule, and regulation that modern society used to grind down people's dignity and rob them of their personal freedom. Yeah, that's right—a God-given mission to fight every damn law, every impersonal rule and strangling regulation that made everyone a malleable state automaton.

A warm feeling came over TJ. With a pulse pounding in his head, TJ declared to no one in particular and shouted into the heavens about his mission. "Humans were born to be free, and I shall deliver a righteous pox on those who make it their duty do otherwise."

Well, stand by, world. One Thaddeus Jones is no damn malleable entity for a social engineering authority to manipulate.

No sir.

Thaddeus Jones is a real-life, freedom-loving individual, and he is coming your way to poke a freedom stick right between your hubris and arrogance. He has the righteous resolve to shove your rules and regulations right into that special place where the sun doesn't dare shine.

CHAPTER 3

TJ and Rajah

Well, surely, you have heard the old saying that for every man there's a woman.

Well, there is a lifer salesman in the used car business, and he says with much authority, "There is an ass for every car seat. All you have to do as a salesman is to find the ass that fits into your fine, rich Corinthian leather, heated car seat."

So too, there must be some earthy wisdom behind the expression "No man is an island," and everyone must somehow have a friend and/or a companion somewhere. All you have to do is find that friend. The fact that everyone has a friend somewhere must be true because even TJ managed to inadvertently acquire a friend.

That's right.

Even TJ had a friend.

Even though he managed to accumulate only one friend throughout life here on earth, he, nevertheless, had a true friend. Because TJ was so different and provocative, he would forever have only one friend.

Well, blessings come in sizes and manner of circumstances.

Most people never manage to accrue even one true friend in life, so it's remarkable that TJ was privileged to have one true friend who would stick with him through thick and thin, even to the grave. It just so happened that TJ's friend was also in Miss Carmichael's class at the time of the alphabet escapade, and his name was Roger Barnabas, or Rajah, as TJ came to call him.

Rajah was just as different from the rest of the students as TJ was.

However, Rajah was not a contrarian questioning everything. No, Rajah was a very structured person with a mind that used logic and reason to place everything into a practical and usable black-and-white relief. Rajah would eventually become a celebrated mathematician and scientist of note, and though he did not suspect it at the time, he would also become a valuable balance and enabler for TJ's "take no prisoners" attitude.

But most of all, Rajah was a friend to TJ because when you hung out with TJ, unexpected and exciting things were always in the making. Rajah was too ordered a person to cause unexpected and exciting things to happen, but when he was with TJ, he could experience things that he could never conjure up alone.

Rajah was amazed and delighted by the alphabet encounter that questioned the authority of the all-mighty teacher. Who on earth other than TJ would have ever thought it was necessary to question why the *a* preceded the *b* in the alphabet?

Who indeed?

And so Rajah treasured the opportunity to be TJ's friend and companion and share an exciting life that he could never have by himself.

As things would develop, TJ and Rajah were destined to be lifelong and cherished friends. And after TJ described his mission to save the world's population from a horrible and depressing induction into a state-run Borg collective, Rajah and TJ swore kinship as blood brothers to rid the world of freedom-robbing tyranny.

TJ and Rajah agreed that in order to make their lifelong friendship a reality, a blood brother ritual would be required to ratify and solidify the bond. Even though both boys had a long way to go in order to complete their formal education, they, nevertheless, were aware of how blood brother rituals were practiced.

So the earnest world savers put their heads together in order to establish a plan to mix their blood and complete the blood brother ritual. First, they thought that Mother Nature had to provide the venue for their coming together in order to sanctify the holy ritual. They both agreed that conducting the ritual in nature seemed to be the only way to satisfy a need for an important witness. The witnesses could not possibly be their parents, so Mother Nature would be the logical choice.

Second, they had to decide what the correct time to do the ritual would be. They agreed that the time they selected had to add to the ritual, bathing the participants in a solemn light. In an inspired flash of agreement, they both said in unison that a full moon would bath the ritual in a soft glow that would enhance the solemn nature of the event.

Thirdly, they concluded, nature in all of its might should be in attendance to add a powerful emphasis to their actions. And one of the best ways for this to happen would only be when nature was in full force, namely during an old-fashioned Indiana thunderstorm.

So they had settled on a plan of action.

But how could make all of these plans happen? That was the question.

This would be the first real test of their competency in their mission to save the world.

They accepted the challenge with relish.

The first solution to come to mind was to join the Boy Scouts and find a way to convince the leadership to agree to have a campout in a selected nature area during a full moon and during a time when a thunderstorm was likely.

It didn't take a great deal of brainpower to quickly decide that making all of the required things happen in an hierarchical organization like the Boy Scouts was well beyond anyone's organizational prowess. Indeed, even Caesar, with complete dictatorial power, could not overcome the hierarchical power of the Roman bureaucracy and the senate.

So after many endless discussions, they eventually realized that in order to stand any chance of success, they would have to somehow involve their parents in the process. They would have to do this without their parents becoming suspicious of their true intent because it was unlikely that their parents would ever agree to a blood brother ritual between TJ and Rajah.

Perhaps with a little planning and a great deal of luck, a family campout in a nature area could coincide with a glorious Indiana full moon and a potential rousing thunder boomer. If all of that could somehow be orchestrated, success just might be possible for their blood brother ceremony. Much time and patience will be required to make the plan feasible and it was not until TJ and Rajah became university students that they had the wherewithal to begin to activate the requirements for the plan.

To get the plan under way, TJ and Rajah carefully considered and scouted out a number of places where nature existed in all of its glory. When they completed their list of appropriate places, they suggested to their respective parents the various places to visit because of a desire for more meaningful family time together.

TJ and Rajah further suggested that their family spend time in nature's backyard by visiting the primal woods that were in abundance in Indiana. That had to be better than going to an amusement park or watching TV together. The clueless parents were trapped by the boy's logic and acquiesced enthusiastically to the suggestions of spending family time in nature.

What responsible parents could resist such as request from their progeny when it was usually the parents who took on the impossible task of finding meaningful things to do as a family that the kids would eagerly agree to.

So with the beaming and enthralled parents fully engaged, the boys visited area after area during available weekends. And then just when it seemed the wheels were about to come off their plan, they found a place that was exceptional. When they arrived at this special place, the boys were pleasantly surprised when their parents expressed their desire to spend more time enjoying nature's bounty, and this place was the perfect place to do just that.

TJ and Rajah concluded the place had potential. And so TJ and Rajah added to the whimsical moment by noisily romping throughout the area to demonstrate their newfound love of nature. With a group hug, all agreed this was a special place, and the boys concluded that this was indeed the perfect place to conduct their blood brother ritual.

The place was deep in old-growth woods in south central Indiana where not so long ago the last continental glacier came to a halt. It was indeed a privileged place. Not only were there old-growth trees in abundance, but there were also critters and much flora that could have been here before humans walked upright upon this land. There was a meandering stream nearby that was busy gurgling over rocks and forest debris on its way to places where nature demanded. Moreover, the place was a part of the Yellow Wood state park system, so public use was encouraged.

The strategy of involving their parents was reinforced by the unexpected behavior of Mom and Pop Jones and Mom and Pop

Barnabas themselves. They were all enjoying the family time spent being together in one of nature's finest venues. Indeed, they have begun to look forward to their family time in the more primitive ecosystems of south central Indiana because it somehow unearthed a latent camaraderie with nature that modern living had been suppressing.

TJ and Rajah now consulted almanacs for moon phases in order to learn the schedule of the full moon, and they gathered meteorological data to determine when thunderstorms were most likely in the selected area of the state.

When they analyzed all of the data, they discovered that a weekend in the middle of July would be the best possible time to have a potential thunder boomer under a full moon.

It was not all that difficult to get their parents to plan a weekend campout on the selected date because they welcomed the promise of a warm summer day or two in their special place. The weekend campout would be a splendid respite from their dehumanizing regimens that modern American businesses now demanded.

The campout had all of the elements required for a fabulous weekend of primitive camping in the woods. With warm weather, the excited and eager participants loaded up the family chariots with tents, food, water, shovels (for latrines and other duties), clothes, hatchets for chopping wood to ensure a rousing campfire, and so on.

The campers arrived at their hallowed ground on a Friday evening, set up tents, ate junk food, and fell fast asleep in their tents after an exhausting day of work and camping preparations.

Tomorrow would be a better day.

And indeed, it was.

The better day was full of adventure, so full that TJ and Rajah nearly forgot why they were here in the first place. Tadpoles, darter minnows, water spiders, and geodes were just a few of the marvelous things they found while wading bare foot in the creek. Musty wood smells, delicate flowers, itchy weeds, a snake or two, and a rare occasion to see a mama deer with spotted fawn in tow capped off a day like no other.

Pop Jones and Pop Barnabas chopped up enough wood and kindling to build a controlled campfire. Mama Jones and Mama Barnabas were busy making dinner when the fire was just right. The smell of burning wood was an intoxicating end to a fantastic day. With full bellies and a zephyr whispering high among the trees, the entourage was content to just enjoy being in a privileged place with family and friends.

TJ and Rajah looked up through the slowly dancing treetops and saw a magnificent full moon shining with all of its childbearing power. Mama Earth's constant companion was riding high among the treetops while some gathering clouds were framing the night sky with picture-perfect artistry.

Excitement was beginning to build when TJ and Rajah began to realize that their complicated plan for the blood brother ritual was already being realized now. All they needed now was a thunder boomer.

Just as the boys were thinking that perhaps a good old-fashioned Indiana thunderstorm might not be all that necessary to complete the blood brother ritual, fate took command.

The fragrant gentle zephyr that had been their friendly companion for the day started to give way to a strengthening wind that began to blow with increasing urgency from the southwest. All looked on as the gathering clouds became more driven and numerous as they changed a bucolic scene, framing the night sky into a dazzling race between moon and clouds. The clouds were now chasing the moon faster and faster through the treetops in a race that would surely end in victory for the clouds.

The gentle zephyr had now morphed into a howling wind that made a noise through the trees that no urbanite had ever hear while ensconced in their three-bedroom ranch or carefree condo.

All hands on deck as the southwest wind increased in velocity and began to trash the tents that the urban campers had set up in nature's privileged domicile.

Poor parents.

They just didn't have the camping skills or correct equipment to set up tents that could withstand a good Indiana thunder boomer now brewing up in the angry southwest sky. With the thunderstorm playing in accordance with orchestral precision, the movement for rain began to pelt the leaves and surrounding area with nature's style of staccato music, and it increased in volume with each passing moment.

The flimsy tents didn't stand a chance against a determined wind. The horizontal rain finished the job of dislodging the store-bought shelters and sent them unceremoniously on their way through the trees and underbrush. As the tents were flying away, a dagger of lighting flashed over the treetops and produced a clap of thunder that took the breath away from the laughing and shouting humans as they ran after their tents.

TJ and Rajah immediately knew that this was the moment they had planned for. They looked at each other in utter bewilderment as they realized that destiny must surely be on their side.

So as the soaked parents were laughing, shouting, and running with glee, when nature took her measure of the out-of-place humans, TJ and Rajah were also running and shouting until they got to a place where a large oak tree hid them from their parents' view. They each took out their sharpened knifes and made a small cut on their respective fingers. As the blood began to flow, it mixed with the rain. It was as if heaven was baptizing the ceremony.

TJ and Rajah pressed their fingers together and mixed their blood.

They were now blood brothers.

They looked up just as the moon found a hole in the clouds. All of a sudden, the world smelled and looked different as a wave of contentment flooded over them much like the heaven-sent rain that was soaking them with righteous and purifying water.

They felt they were special and blessed.

TJ and Rajah were now blood brothers with a need to define their impossible mission to restore sovereign man to his rightful place. They decided that their goal was to bring forth the real Age of Aquarius so that all people could live in peace and harmony as free and sovereign human beings.

Such a mission and goal might seem ambitious to normal humans, but bear in mind that the American Revolution was precipitated by just a handful of men and supported by less than 2 percent of the population. And as a result of such courageous and dangerous activity, the world became a much better place not only for future freedom-loving Americans but also for the entire world of huddled masses yearning to be free.

So we now have a contrarian and a nerd bound together in common cause as blood brothers, vowing to revitalize the notion that only sovereign humans can be worthy of the life so freely given by a gracious God or splendid nature.

Perhaps you noticed a similarity between the goal of TJ and Rajah and that of the first American Revolution. You know, the first American Revolution that resulted in the adoption of the final US Constitution that codified the same values and purpose that TJ and Rajah have now vowed to restore.

One can only speculate as to why the American Revolution began to sputter and brought us to a point where nowadays we live with a dehumanizing governmental machine instead of a government "of the people, by the people, and for the people." Where have all of the freedom-loving sovereign people gone? Well, a few of them are still out there, and TJ and Rajah are among their diminishing numbers. And their vista has demanded haste in their holy undertaking in order to prevent the last remaining laissez-faire humans from becoming extinct artifacts just like the magnificent Mastodon that used to reign stately over this land. Hopefully, the last remaining sovereign humans might even rise to the 2 percent mark of the last exceptional revolution to provide some aid and comfort to our patriotic duo.

TJ and Rajah will become the modern-age Quixote and Panza fighting hopeless odds to wage holy war against a well-entrenched governmental establishment that claws at people in order to turn them into obedient state-directed automatons to populate their contemptible idea of utopia.

Their choice of weapons in the righteous fight to come will not be lances, guns, or clinched fists. Oh, no, the fearsome weapon they will bring onto the field of battle will be their combined intellect, using the government bureaucracy against itself.

Consider one of the twenty-six war strategies suggested by the Chinese: "Kill with a borrowed sword." This strategy recommended using someone else to fight your battles. TJ and Rajah intend to use this strategy, and they would use the sword they borrowed to hack the bloated government back down to constitutional size.

TJ and Rajah believed such a strategy had a beautiful and symbolic symmetry. They would use the hand that strangled them to strangle their perpetrators.

Beautiful symmetry or not, TJ and Rajah would be the ones who defined the battlefield and the weapons they used, not the bloated fat-cats of the governmental nightmare. The modern-day heroes would from this day forward sally forth on their mission to save the world from the modern utopian nightmare. But unfortunately, they would also suffer a lack of cooperation. The general population was too busy texting, tweeting and Facebooking one another to become all that concerned with things like government-manufactured automatons.

However, they would have to wait until they had satisfied the requirements of becoming fully educated. Mom and Pop Jones as well as Mr. and Mrs. Barnabas were quite firm about their boys being educated in the modern way, even though TJ thought organized education was more about indoctrination than education. Rajah was certainly more enthusiastic about becoming educated than the ambivalent and contrarian TJ, who looked at any organized activity with a suspicious eye.

In fact, Rajah rather enjoyed being inundated with facts, wherefores, whereases, therefores, and especially numbers. These things brought a glowing personal satisfaction that TJ could never experience. While social studies and other similar subjects were interesting, Rajah had such an aptitude for all things mathematics that he soaked like a junkie on drugs.

Rajah had such a passion and talent for math that it was not uncommon for him to have a more advanced knowledge of the mathematical concepts that the math professors laboriously lectured to him and his peers. Of course, Rajah was too polite and respectful of his teachers to ever use his inherent math knowledge to embarrass his teachers or peers for that matter.

On the other hand, TJ treated math like it was a plague. He believed math was invented by devious men bent on controlling as much of mankind as they could. Math, according to TJ, was a man-made disease designed to condition growing young human brains so that they became susceptible to programmed thoughts.

TJ further believed that a brain conditioned and altered by math would then be ripe for utopian programming, such as social justice and other such doctrinaire nonsense. Such programming would then produce doddering humans that would follow instructions with German like precision in order to populate their manufactured society as state-directed automatons.

A math-programmed mind would be the ultimate tool for tyrants to advance their goal of turning mankind into malleable automatons. They do this, according to TJ, by programming the young math-conditioned brains through the modern education process, and then adults acquiescent to group thought and state authority.

So said TJ.

Rajah was too polite and respectful of TJ to point out that he, too, was the proud possessor of a brain that had been chocked full of math programming. However, Rajah did point out that the likelihood that he could become a state directed automaton was as likely as Vladimir Putin directing that the Russian Patriotic State Band to strike up a rousing extravaganza of The Stars And Stripes Forever.

And by the way, just in case there was a smidgeon of truth in TJ's rant about math being a cloaked mole bent on turning sovereign beings into revolting automatons, being TJ's friend would certainly insulate him from such a wicked fate in any event.

CHAPTER 4

Malicious Compliance

TJ and Rajah were feeling empowered now that they were full-fledged blood brothers. However, they found it more and more difficult to spend time together to discuss how they were going to go forward with their quest to lead the people back to the constitutional future. The university demanded that all their attention be diverted exclusively to their studies. Their full regimen of study sharply curtailed any spare time for serious discussions on how to take down the all-mighty government.

Mom and Pop Jones as well as Mr. and Mrs. Barnabas all demanded complete fidelity to their university studies, and any reports of excessive social activity was met with somber discussions at the kitchen table.

The blood brothers both agreed that the university was taking all their precious time, but the time was providing a much broader foundation of understanding, especial governmental history in particular.

As part of that broader understanding, TJ found the writings of Marcus Tullius Cicero (106–43 BC) to be inspiring, and Cicero's treatise on law (51 BC) was of supreme interest. Cicero's treatise not only connected God and nature to man's requirement for law; it was the basis of understanding for many of our country's founding fathers as they formulated the foundations of our government and then codified that understanding within the constitution of the United States of America.

TJ and Rajah both found joy in discussing all the finer details of Cicero's treatise on law, and they decided that they would conduct any further discussions on how to achieve their mission in the same manner as Cicero had done with his brothers Quintus and Atticus. Marcus Cicero always held his discussions in a grove that was near the River Liris. And in that grove was a mighty and ancient oak tree. In the shade of that oak tree is where Cicero conducted his discussions about law. Perhaps Cicero selected that location because the stately and ancient oak tree could serve as a visual symbol that law, too, was the stuff of longevity and stately existence.

While TJ and Rajah would have loved to have their discussions under a mighty and ancient oak tree in the forest where they had consummated their blood brother ritual, the location of the forest and fickle Indiana weather prevented them from considering the location.

Instead they selected a location in the basement of TJ parents' house. Old furniture went there to die a dignified death, but his parents allowed it to serve as TJ's man cave. The basement location was also where TJ and his friends could have some private space without nosy parents butting in. It was in this basement sanctuary that TJ and Rajah had their discussions about girls, unfair university rules, the price of dates, stupid Democrats and Republicans, and of course, how to save the world from becoming a Borg collective.

The basement did not quite have the same gravitas as Cicero, Quintus, and a mighty oak tree, but the location did offer a musty basement smell along with cobweb-filtered light flickering from a basement window that was last cleaned before TJ's birth.

And instead of sitting firmly on Mother Earth's unforgiving terra firma, an old leather sofa provided a well-worn and forgiving seat. However, a spring or two would make its presence known to a backside that did not shift positions occasionally. From this position, one could take up the weighty opinions and lofty ideals that were somewhat worthy of Cicero and Quintus.

There was also a well-worn armchair in that basement that would have felt right at home in the household of Archie Bunker, even with one leg askew. The armchair had faithfully recorded all the history of spilled drinks, slopped food, and many other things long before the area became a man cave. For some reason, this armchair became the unrestricted venue from which Rajah would face his blood brother and provide point and counterpoint to the strident assertions of TJ.

So on one Saturday night—their nights were usually free because they didn't have girlfriends willing to go dutch on dates with the political nerds—TJ started a conversation based on the writings of Machiavelli.

TJ squirmed on his sofa and began by saying, "I believe it was Niccolo Machiavelli who wrote in his 1513 tome, *The Prince*, 'What doctors say about consumption applies here.' At the beginning the disease is easy to cure but difficult to diagnose, but in the course of time, when it was not diagnosed at first and treated, it becomes easy to diagnose but difficult to cure. Thus, it happens in the affairs of state. If the evils that are developing are diagnosed from afar, which only the prudent man can do, they are quickly cured, but when they have not been diagnosed and are allowed to grow so that everyone recognizes them, then there is no longer any remedy for them."

TJ was in agreement with the misunderstood Machiavelli, whose metaphor about how the unchecked disease of tuberculosis would bring about the ultimate destruction of the human body, and the ultimate destruction of the citizen body politic by the unchecked disease of governmental tyranny was spot on.[5]

TJ believed that all governments by virtue of what they are and how they must operate are all equally created with a liberty-destroying germ encoded within their modus operandi, and the germ cannot be destroyed without destroying the government itself. However, much like the germ of consumption can be controlled at its early stage by careful medical therapy administered by knowledgeable doctors, likewise, the germ of governmental tyranny can be controlled by careful hegemony therapy administered by knowledgeable liberty-loving citizens.

And furthermore, if responsible citizens do not administer hegemony therapy constantly, in time the unchecked tyranny germ will easily overwhelm the governmental will of the people, for the people, and by the people. Then governmental tyranny is incurable at this point, and the only remedy remaining for the people is the destruction of the government itself because it has it becomes an enemy of the people rather than their servant.

These are some of the discussions that TJ and Rajah were having while trying to decide on a course of action to cure governmental tyranny by the liberty-loving citizens of today.

TJ thought that government tyranny was already beyond the point of curing, so dismantling and reconstituting the constitutional government was the only solution available in his

---

[5] Most modern people who have never bothered to read *The Prince* misunderstand Machiavelli and so believe the idea that is encouraged by his writing is the notion that "the end justifies the means" in government. However, careful reading of *The Prince* will reveal that Machiavelli wrote how one could rule by despotic means if they so desired. But he (Machiavelli) always pointed out that this way of governing was doomed to eventual failure and should not be pursued because despotic rule by tyrants is not only immoral, it will always fail as well.

opinion. Only then, he believed, would it be practical and possible to restore to the original US Constitution.

Rajah, being the ever-cautious and calculating person he was, rejoined, "I believe that trying to dismantle the current government is not only impossible, but it's exceedingly dangerous as well."

TJ immediately responded with the Thomas Jefferson quote "The tree of liberty must be refreshed from time to time with the blood of patriots and tyrants."

TJ further made it clear what he believed the true meaning of the Thomas Jefferson quote was. "If you believe that personal freedom and liberty for all is not important enough to die for, then tyranny can never be defeated by ordinary citizens because a corrupt government will render the ballot box and all other means ineffective for citizens to control governmental activity."

After much consideration, Rajah replied, "TJ, you are as right as rain if indeed the current situation was dire enough to demand such drastic and deadly action. The reality is that ordinary citizens are much too busy as enterprising and productive private persons living their daily lives to pay all that much attention to government activity, unless, of course, it becomes obvious and personal. And it only becomes obvious and personal when government activity is causing their catastrophic and personal suffering."

Rajah continued on, "Indeed, this is exactly the reason why the founding fathers framed this country as a democratic republic rather than a pure democracy. Our elected and appointed representatives were supposed to be selected in order to look after citizen affairs in government because we as free and productive citizens are much too busy pursuing our personal affairs to constantly monitor government goings on. This defines and gives dimension to the notion of freedom and liberty for ordinary citizens. This is also the circumstance that tyrannical government exploits to further its inexhaustible lust for power, which is nowadays aided and abetted by the professional politicians we have elected to look after our affairs instead of electing citizen legislators. The professional politicians look after their own professional well being rather than that of the citizens who elected them. They do this even though the professional politicians gave their solemn oath to preserve and protect the constitution and the freedom of the citizens. In this regard, the professional politicians we elect aid and abet the tyrannical government we so despise. Nevertheless, I don't think we yet reached the stage yet where ordinary citizens in desperation will pick up their pitchforks and clubs to join us in order to remove the tyrants from power, which, by the way, also includes the professional politicians who are so disgustingly corrupt. And that only leaves the two of us to do the job, which would be as daunting as me challenging God to a duel in a contest for power."

A prolonged silence punctuated the wisdom of Rajah as each considered what they could do to get their holy crusade off the ground. Without offering agreement or disagreement, TJ cleared his throat and mind to offer up a possible strategy that might be a viable way to get this thing rolling.

TJ presented a real-life allegory that was relayed to him some time ago by a disconsolate senior who had labored most of his adult life in a corporate environment. Perhaps this senior's experience in the impersonal and dehumanizing corporate world might point to a way to deal with our impersonal and dehumanizing government world as well.

The fellow relating his experiences in corporate America was a practicing and successful engineer, and he relayed his story about what a professional engineer must do in order to manage to survive as working-class professionals in the new and improved America.

Note that that the term used was *manage* instead of *lead*. Leading instead of managing is, of course, the total quality management (TQM) way to do business as espoused by the eminent American Dr. W. Edwards Deming. Dr. Deming outlined his principles in his tour de force *Out of the Crisis*, namely those used by the postwar Japanese as the blueprint for their very successful business model.

As so often happens in modern America, seminal work like Dr. Deming's is ignored by American business as they plod their way onward to the next Wall Street mandated quarterly balance sheet. What is so embarrassing is that American business could not understand that the business model the Japanese were using to become so successful was a business model that took advantage of Dr. Deming's principles. (Just ask the American automobile manufacturing industry.)

Of course, there is a perpetrator of this American business malfeasance, and that being American Academy, and in particular, the Harvard Business School along with numerous lesser-known academic brethren. The new and improved Harvard-inspired American business way being of course, the Wall Street mandated quarterly balance sheet. The quarter balance sheet is now the Holy Grail that signifies business success with little regard to quality or anything else that smacks of business.

The holy quarterly balance sheet, which is the lifeblood of the Wall Street moneymakers, is now the determining factor that beguiles business success or failure. And that balance sheet is rapidly overtaking the invisible hand of the free marketplace and changing capitalism from an engine of productive enterprise into a gambler's system of beating the odds in the stock market casino.

Yes, the Harvard business school churns out snot-nose experts who march into corporate America with their inexperienced steely eyes firmly fixated on the quarterly balance sheet. Making money off of money is surely not the Adam Smith definition of productive enterprise and the true building block for the wealth of a nation.

By the way, the typical Harvard know-it-alls, most of who have never done a productive thing or gotten their hands dirty in their entire adolescent lives, are now the managers of American business. (If only God would point his finger down at Harvard University and cause a giant sinkhole to swallow up the entire enterprise, this magnificent country might have a fiddler's chance of becoming productive and great again.)

Well, onward with the allegory of the modern-day engineer doing time in corporate prime. Professional engineer Joe Doaks was not only a man of considerable experience, skill, and ability in the applied physical sciences, he was also a man who had a keen sense of integrity. He served a purpose greater than that of corporate servitude and the hubris of his employer. He had a professional moral compass to maintain a personal and professional reputation that was second to none.

As is often the case, when one is required to march in step with the corporate direction, dealing with hard physical science, good engineering practice, and corporate weenies all at the same time is something that King Solomon would not be able to successfully navigate.

So there came a day when the sun was shining brightly, the kids where safely off to school, and all was right within the Doaks universe, Engineer Joe Doaks buckled up for just another day of putting bread on the table. Arriving at his home away from home, Engineer Joe Doaks reached into his "In" basket for the latest communications, be they technical, corporate or otherwise.

As was his early morning routine, Engineer Doaks was first attending to the requirements of the "In" basket so that he could get to work on important engineering matters. Engineer Doaks was a veteran of memo reading and was quickly dispatching memo after memo when he stopped short after quickly reading a memo from some corporate assistant.

Engineer Doaks was not only a good engineer he was also a cautious man. And the cautious man stopped to carefully reread the memo that grabbed his attention. Engineer Doaks slowly put the memo down, leaned back in his swivel chair and fixed his gaze at the ceiling. Engineer Doaks was carefully going over all of the ramifications of the memo in his orderly mind.

After careful consideration, Engineer Joe Doaks carefully replied to the memo directly without going through the normal chain of command. The reply respectfully pointed out to the corporate weenies how their enlightened memorandum would make it impossible to comply with good engineering practice to continue producing a quality product, which would undoubtedly result in unhappy customers.

This was a bad move.

Upon receiving the unsolicited reply by Engineer Doaks, the higher-ups immediately circled the corporate wagons and had meetings with intermediate management with instructions to stamp out the insubordination with haste, lest it spread to the proletariat masses. And furthermore, management was directed to point out to Mr. Joe Doaks that his being at odds with corporate would label him a troublemaker with plenty of negative ramifications.

So here is a dichotomy in practice. Engineer Joe Doaks knew shit rolled downhill, and he lived in the corporate valley, so he did what most of us would do. He put on a metaphorical hard hat to deflect the shit raining down upon his righteous head. He created a situation where his good engineering practice could continue, thus protecting his customer and his job while creating all kinds of visible movement so that it appeared he was in accordance with the corporate directives.

This is inspired knowledge put to practical use, and it comes from years of experience. The inspired knowledge being that the corporate weenies cannot distinguish between motion and activity.

Engineer Joe Doaks did all of this to convince the insular corporate world that he was following their directives to the letter. Joe Doak's project was running smoothly, apparently in accordance with management's dumb-ass directives. However, in reality, he was continuing his best engineering practices to ensure success, but this was hidden from the corporate weenies by means of fake enthusiasm and phony affirmative head shaking, thus acting out the self-serving Kabuki drama.

But of course, the real responsibility for the success or failure of the project cannot be assigned in reality. If the project fails, corporate says it's the result of unenthusiastic compliance to management's directives by the insubordinate engineers, and so the responsibility for failure rests with the engineer. If the project goes smoothly, it's because the directives were followed in spite of the carping by the engineer, and success validates corporate meddling in engineering affairs.

As you can see, the dichotomy ensures a win-win situation for the corporate weenies and a lose-lose scenario for the working stiff who actually has to do the job. So what happens? As time goes by, altercations with management solidify the righteous engineer's identity as a troublemaker, even while he and his team are laboriously managing to maintain success along with good engineering practices.

This situation creates much unneeded strife and premature gray hair.

So in a burst of divine inspiration, it occurred to Mr. Joe Doaks that in order for the shit to stop raining down upon him, malicious compliance should become the order of the day.

Whenever the corporate weenies issued a bonehead directive, he would enthusiastically comply with it now, and he would let the engineering chips fall where they may. By so doing, he could maliciously wreck his good engineering practices, but the responsibility for failure has a fighting chance of being placed where it rightfully belongs.

With nearly celestial certainty, the uncontested compliance with the corporate direction would result in engineering failure, but now the cause of failure could not be Engineer Joe Doak's. After all, he followed corporate orders to the letter. Malicious compliance was now the new and improved hard hat that would protect a righteous engineer from malevolent corporate punishment.

When the project failed because of the bonehead directives, even management would see it was not because of insubordination by the drone worker bee. If the project was a success, it was probably because the directives were not able to screw up regular work. All in all, it was a win for Engineer Doaks and everyone else associated with the project.

And if Mr. Doaks followed the directives faithfully and enthusiastically—at least in appearance—and the project still failed, perhaps the corporate weenie who issued the dumb-ass directive could be held responsible for the project's failure.

But corporate weenies did not ascend to corporate heights by acknowledging their own malfeasance. The only time corporate weenies demonstrate creativity is when they are required to assess blame, which is mostly shifted to innocent persons, and to list all of the conditions beyond their control.

It is truly unfortunate that our workplaces have transitioned from professional to personal, but welcome to the real world. It should be noted that after malicious compliance became the order of the day, enginner Joe Doaks was repeatedly awarded raises and advancement. But of course, the sad result of all of this was that this corporate enterprise would become noncompetitive and fall into ruin, as it always must whenever management becomes insular and top heavy. Productive enterprise is wasted by hubris, and productive enterprise is the only measure of success in a free market.

And because we are dealing with reality here, it must be reported that righteous engineer Joe Doaks was still done in by corporate hubris. This is the sad but true tale of engineer Joe Doaks.

A new manager was assigned to engineer Doak's work group, and this snot-nose manager, wanting to establish his management bona fides, insisted that he must approve all written communications. Therefore, in accordance with the new administrative requirement, Mr. Doaks dutifully forwarded a routine letter to his customer detailing project status to Mr. Snot Nose.

Mr. Snot Nose made a number of "corrections and suggestions" in red on the letter and returned the letter to Mr. Doaks for revision. With reluctance, Mr. Doaks complied with all of the marks and resubmitted the letter again to Mr. Snot Nose. Mr. Snot Nose bled on the revised letter again and returned the said letter to Mr. Doaks for further revision.

This back and forth between righteous engineer and snot-nose manager went on for thirteen iterations until Mr. Doaks submitted the original unedited letter in total disgust. Upon receiving the original letter, Mr. Snot Nose approved the letter, and the blessed letter sailed off into customer land.

Mr. Joe Doaks turned in his resignation the very next day and retired from engineering duty. Management was clueless as to why such a valued engineer and rewarded employee had so abruptly quit.

So TJ asked rhetorically, "Could malicious compliance be the borrowed sword to hack our government back down to constitutional size?"

Rajah paused to reflect upon the delightful story TJ had offered as a possible guide on how to use the government's own rules, regulations, directives, and God only know whatever as a borrowed sword.

Rajah pointed out, "Your story about how a righteous engineer managed to deal with an insular corporate world that thinks workers are just functional pieces that their Harvard-trained management can move about at will to achieve success is spot on. The Harvard emphasis on corporate management success rather than teaming with the workers to achieve business success is a sad commentary. The problem, as I see it, is the corporate world. While similar to that of any government body, it is not comparable to the size, scope, and manner of existence of government. And these differences will make the method of malicious compliance impossible to implement in an effective manner."

Rajah reluctantly continued on, "Most importantly, as I see it, by using one of the Chinese war strategies, we have now signified an acceptance of the notion that a citizen *war* is the only way to deal with the implacable behemoth called the collective local, state, and federal government. This acceptance of *war* is a milestone of considerable importance in that we now agree upon a strategy to prosecute our endeavor, and so we now can concentrate upon facilitating the tactical means to do so."

Rajah was warming up and further declared, "The tactical problem is that the enemy collective government has now become, in large measure, a mindless bureaucracy that doesn't respond to any outside force, legal or otherwise. When bureaucracy becomes insular incarnate, it also becomes nearly immune to attack by any outside force. It's sort of like trying to move Jell-O with a toothpick."

Rajah continued on, "Even an administration that created a bureaucracy to do its bidding becomes hostage to the embedded boys and girls who cling to power and position like barnacles that fastens themselves to the bottom of a well-designed boat. For confirmation, I repeat that even Caesar with unlimited dictatorial power could not overcome the Roman bureaucracy and senate."

Rajah also pointed out, "The present-day situation mirrors, in a remarkable way, the same kind of insular bureaucracy that was responsible in large part for the ruin of the Roman Empire."

"Good Lord," exclaimed Rajah. "If Caesar couldn't bend the Roman bureaucracy to his will and save Rome, how on earth would a modern-day contrarian and math nerd sally forth on their righteous constitutional steeds to battle a bureaucracy blob that smoothers the entire modern landscape.

After a pause, Rajah mused, "The American bureaucracy has become a ubiquitous smothering blob that strangely must look like the endless regiments of windmills that Don Quixote and Panza rode out to battle in order to restore chivalry."

A very serious Rajah further pointed out, "The mindless bureaucracy blob is in reality more like the monster hydra that only grows more heads for every head you hack off with your righteous borrowed sword.

"And today's battle will be much more complicated than that of Quixote riding to battle the windmills that only mangled his lance as he thrust it into the whirling blades. Today's battle will surely not only mangle your righteous borrowed sword but will, like a hydra, grow more departments to deal with your outside meddling, and then it will destroy you as well. And it will do all of these things with mindless bureaucracy efficiency and indifference.

"So it is difficult to see how malicious compliance can be adapted to our tactics of bring a wayward government to heel so that sovereign humans can live in peace and harmony."

All TJ could muster up to respond was, "What the hell? This is far too complicated to be effective. Let's instead rally the righteous citizens to grab their pitchforks and clubs, and then we will physically remove the lot of them."

Rajah breathed a sigh of relief.

CHAPTER 5

Because It's the Law

TJ and Rajah were busy with family, jobs, education, and friends while their righteous mission awaited their next move. Next move or not, what was about to happen on a remote stretch of American highway would provide dimension to the scope of their sacred mission and the problems associated therein.

While en route to a university-sponsored seminar on how CO_2 is destroying the planet, the mind-numbing incident took place.

But wait. You may not understand how a citadel of advanced learning could promote a seminar on how CO_2, what humans exhale, is hurting Mother Earth. Well, let us examine the ways.

The Environmental Protection Agency (EPA), aided and abetted by the almighty Supreme Court of these United States, has declared that CO_2 is a pollutant, and the declared pollutant is destroying our gracious Mother Earth. CO_2 does this by means of its heat-trapping properties. The pollutant CO_2 is trapping heat and thereby causing a buildup of heat that would normally escape into the cosmos.

This situation is thereby causing our climate to change and become hotter. And the temperature will increase until life itself is in jeopardy. And furthermore, the CO2 pollutant is generated by man's activity on the planet.

Wait for it.

After all, humans exhale CO2. It follows that exhaling humans and all of their activities must somehow be restrained in order to save the planet. Now who doesn't want to save the planet for our children and grandchildren? Lucky for us, the government will reluctantly expand its power in order to control all things human. In their eyes humans are the ones causing this catastrophe, and by so regulating them, the government can save the planet for us all.

But wait. There's more.

Because humans love to eat meat and raise cattle, our obscene meat-eating nature is causing further planetary ruin.

How?

Well, it turns out that the bovine we slaughter for McDonald's hamburgers are also the same cows that comes off our barbie as a warm and juicy steak that we enthusiastically stab with our steely knifes. Now we've all seen cattle eating all of the vegetation within reach in order to grow big enough for us humans to eat. Well, something else happens when the cattle eat all of that vegetation. The innocent and peaceful bovines expel a gas as a by-product of the digestive process.

That gas is called *flatulence.*

Now the subject may be unpleasant, but your government thinks this is important, so let's all stick together on this.

The flatulence expelled by the grazing cattle contains methane, a gas rich in CO2, and it is an even more potent greenhouse gas than CO2. Therefore, it is obvious to enlightened and gullible citizens alike that humans raising cattle to eat is another factor contributing greatly to catastrophic climate change.

How could us dumb-butt humans do such a thing?

But of course, all things green on Earth need CO2 to grow, and when they grow, they produce a by-product called oxygen. Oxygen is a gas that provides animals, such as humans, cattle, and even power-hungry politicians with life.

But who cares about such nonsense when we are saving the planet?

Well, TJ and Rajah were enjoying a good time reliving all that the learned professors had presented concerning human-driven climate change while driving home back from the university-sponsored seminar.

You know, the professional and tenured professors eager to support the government position on human caused climate change because feasting at the government money trough is as good as it gets. And who really cares if scientific and professional ethics get bent a little.

So while returning from the university seminar, TJ was manning the helm of a transplant Japanese small chariot that was effortlessly sailing down a German-inspired Autobahn that we call an interstate.

The transplant chariot also being a major contributor to man caused climate change in so many ways. You know, the cup holder bedecked, heated-seat, air-conditioned, small 4-cylinder high-revving-engine chariot, that was sipping black gold from the sands of Saudi Arabia, that was transported to America by a Panamanian flagged Super Tanker, that was transported via a high-pressure pipeline, much like the evil planet destroying Keystone Pipeline, that was delivered to a planet destroying refinery at an undisclosed location, that was delivered by another evil high pressure pipeline to a midwestern distribution center, that was then transported by an cigar smoking Owner Operator Trucker transport, that delivered state certified 87 octane gasoline to Billy Bobs Service Station Emporium, and then pumped into said transplant Japanese Chariot by one Rajah, because he had the only credit card that would be approved by whirling computers that used planet orbiting satellite relays, god only knows whatever computer links, that sustains the known and unknown virtual financial systems, that was delivered for our use by the mega-conglomerate global moneymakers who could care less about climate change.

TJ was so distracted by the revelry of the climate change seminar that he had been driving on the left high-speed lane of a separated four-lane interstate highway when he should have driving on the right.

When TJ finally realized his driving error, he glanced at his Indy 500 inspired rearview mirror, determined that there was no traffic within visual range, and nudged his speeding vehicle onto the starboard lane.

There was no traffic ahead or behind, so TJ and Rajah continued talking about their recollections of the seminar, unaware that a county sheriff who was hidden behind a grove of hickory trees was finishing up a bag of chili cheese corn chips by Frito Lay while comfortably ensconced in his Ford V-8 police interceptor.

The sheriff deputy, who was known simply as Buford, noticed TJ's lane-changing maneuver. Whereupon deputy sheriff Buford, calmly and with deliberate speed, calmly adjusted his big-brimmed sheriff hat in his rearview mirror, wiped his chili cheese hands on his county-issued uniform, tighten his seat belt around his Frito enhanced belly, checked his Glock 40mm sidearm, raised up to clear his handcuffs from underneath his ample butt, switched on his multi-colored flashing light bar, lovingly flicked on his wa-wa siren while pausing just a moment to savor the sound, and radiocd in he was in a highway pursuit of an older brown Toyota Corolla for a traffic violation. Deputy Buford dropped the big block V-8 into drive, smacked his right pointy toe cowboy boot hard down on the accelerator, kicked up an impressive amount of lose impediments from his spinning rear wheels, and gave authorized chase to an unaware TJ and Rajah.

TJ and Rajah were having a really good laugh while recalling Professor Blow Hard's position that farting cows would lead us all to climate Armageddon when TJ noticed the flashing lights of a police cruiser coming hard up on his stern. TJ thought there must have been an accident ahead, slowed down, turned his right turn signal on, and carefully pulled off onto the highway shoulder to let the speeding vehicle safely pass.

Imagine their surprise when the police land yacht with Deputy Buford at the helm, tossed out the four wheel oversize disc brake anchor and with a billowing dust cloud settling over both vehicles, pulled up directly behind them with his flashing lights and wa-wa siren still going strong. TJ looked at Rajah, and Rajah looked and TJ. And they both said in unison, "What the hell did we do?"

Instinctually looking at his speedometer, TJ proclaimed, "I wasn't speeding. I was only going sixty-five in a seventy zone." TJ continued looking at his zero registering speedometer as if it could confirm his lawful previous speed.

Of all things, Rajah looked at the at speedometer and also proclaimed, "I feel certain you were not exceeding the speed limit."

They had plenty of time to speculate as to the nature of their highway transgression because Deputy Buford was still in his seat busy with police details. Office Buford was radioing in the license plate number of the old brown Corolla and his location on the highway. Officer Buford then punched in the license plate number and car description on his computer to determine if any prior warrants were in effect for the possible desperados who were arm waving at each other in the pulled over car.

In accordance with a ruling of the unelected almighty Supreme Court of these United States, some judges made a decision out of thin air—one that proclaimed whenever a police officer stopped a US citizen for any probable violation, such as a broken brake light, the officer can lawfully search the person and, in this case, the car of the suspected lawbreaker to determine if any other laws have been violated. And with the countless local, state, and federal rules and regulations on the books, the possibilities for breaking the law become endless. Police power rivals that of the Gestapo.

Lucky for TJ and Rajah, the industrial-size package of chili cheese corn chips that Officer Buford had consumed mellowed out the deputy so that he was not all that interested in searching their pathetic little Toyota for additional violations. This was especially so after headquarters reported back over the radio that there were no red flags with the license plate or the person who owned the car.

So Deputy Buford straighten his sheriff's hat once again, looked in rearview mirror to see if any traffic was coming from behind, adjusted his Glock 40 sidearm in its holster, opened his door, and moseyed up to the driver side of the brown Corolla.

Deputy Buford had a warm feeling spreading down his legs as he confirmed that his massive Ford V-8 interceptor dwarfed that of the pathetic 4-banger little brown Toyota Corolla. Upon arriving at the drivers side of the Corolla, he Deputy rolled his hand at the occupants and tapped on the window, thereby instructing said occupant to roll down the window.

Officer Buford was not at all surprised when TJ hand cranked the window down in a herky-jerky manner instead of a smooth power assist crank that a more expensive car had as standard equipment. TJ looked up at the massive deputy with hardware hanging from every possible place only to see his scrawny, pathetic face reflected in the officer's prized mirrored sunglasses.

TJ's butt hole tightened up significantly at the sight.

Officer Buford instructed in his best professional voice, "License and registration, please."

TJ said, "Why did you pull me over? I wasn't doing anything wrong."

Officer Buford repeated in a slightly agitated voice, "License and registration, please."

TJ grumbled while searching franticly for the car registration so that he could comply with a deputy who was growing impatient. TJ finally found the out-of-date registration and handed it to Officer Buford. Unfortunately, TJ dropped his wallet while trying to retrieve his valid driver's license. TJ bending down to get his wallet off the floor caused Officer Buford to instinctually reach for his sidearm. Rajah saw this move by the deputy and carefully instructed TJ to move slowly in a non-threatening manner because the officer had his hand on his gun.

TJ's butt hole cinched up another notch or two.

TJ spilled the contents of his overfilled wallet and only then found his driver's license. He presented it to Officer Buford as instructed, and the deputy carefully examined the registration and license against the information he had received on his computer about the car and its occupant. When Officer Buford was satisfied that all was in order, he handed the two documents back to a somewhat relieved TJ.

Officer Buford reluctantly removed his hand from his trusty sidearm, and in a practiced move, he slowly and deliberately dislodged his sunglasses from his slightly bulbous nose. It was clear he had practiced this move for maximum dramatic effect. He then looked directly at TJ and said, "Mr. Jones, I notice your registration is out of date and therefore invalid."

TJ was caught red-handed and defensively replied, "Well, you would have never known if you hadn't pulled me over for God only knows what."

Rajah's butt hole also tightened up significantly in anticipation of an escalating confrontation with an officer of the law. Not only did this man have all of the power, but he had a very big gun as well.

Deputy Buford was not accustomed to having pipsqueak citizens bark back at him, particularly after all of his intimidating moves had been executed to perfection. The intimidated citizen should have been soiling himself instead of mouthing off at this point.

So the guardian of the law was a little more than annoyed by the two nerds in the little Corolla questioning his authority and judgment. Deputy Sheriff Buford intended to rise to the challenge and nip this insolence in the bud.

The deputy straighten up to full height and authority to signal that business was about to change from a respectful exchange of information to a more pointed command-and-control situation. Deputy Buford increased the volume and bass of his voice to its most commanding tone and said, "Well, young man, I was only going to issue you a warning about your invalid registration, but now I have been forced to amend that unwise decision. I am now going to award your disrespect for the law with a full citation."

TJ looked at Rajah and asked in a pleading voice, "What the hell did I do to warrant this?"

Officer Buford stifled a knowing chuckle at his apparent success. But that success was about to elude the fearless deputy when TJ barked back, "I demand to know why in the hell you pulled me when I know I have not committed a violation of the any law."

A shade of deepening red quickly spread unabated over the officer's entire face. All of the department training about how to respectfully interact with the body citizen went out the window. Officer Buford placed both of his huge farm molded hands on the door of the Corolla, leaned over, and with a chili cheese breath shouted, "Hey, you little shit, I am all the law you need to know about, and you are about to get your shitty little self into a whole lot of trouble."

Rajah's butt hole was now fully locked.

Officer Buford continued, "Because you must have a university inspired little mind, I'll tell you why I pulled you over. I pulled you over because you failed to signal a lane change when you went from the passing lane to the right lane. And rest assured that you and your big mouth will most certainly be getting a ticket for not only a registration violation, but now I will also ticket you for failure to signal a lane change."

Both TJ and Rajah were stunned.

In a somewhat more respectful tone, TJ rebutted, "Officer, I looked in my rearview mirror for traffic behind me and saw none, and I looked ahead for traffic and saw none in sight, so I just changed lanes. The point being, there was no traffic around me to signal to, so I thought there was no need to signal a lane change."

A fully indignant officer of the law paused. He could not quite understand the incomprehensible dumbness of this citizen staring back at him. He then composed himself, leaned his head into the Corolla as far as his department-issued sheriff's hat would allow, and with spittle issuing forth that would do Coach Cowher proud, sputtered, "You know-it-all little shit, how is it that you're so smart and you can't even comprehend the fact that you broke the law. Don't you get it? It's the law that says you must signal a lane change. The law says nothing about you, the driver of a shitty little car, making a judgment as to when you should signal a lane change, only that you should always signal a lane change."

With an even louder voice and with ample spittle to further emphasize the fact, Deputy Buford blasted, "It's the law. Damn it!"

TJ and Rajah both looked at the turn signal lever as if trying to understand how such an innocent little device could get them in so much trouble.

Rajah involuntarily thought back to the second part of Shakespeare's *Henry VI*, where Jack Cade, who hates lawyers, makes somewhat the same point about sheep skin instead of an innocent turn signal lever. "Is not this a lamentable thing, that of the skin of an innocent lamb should be made parchment? That parchment, being scribbled o'er, should undo a man?"

Shakespeare or not, Officer Buford was preparing to remove his hat with the full intention of ordering the two nerds to get out of the car so that they could place their hands on the hood of the car for further inspection.

However, fate interceded at this precise moment.

But first, some context is required.

Not so long ago, on these very same interstate and other highways, big-rig truckers had great sport whenever they spotted an officer of the law pulled off the highway while attending to a citizen's requirement. I guess driving a big rig all day and night every day and night can get rather boring, and so they needed sport to relieve the boredom.

So when the truckers spotted an officer doing his duty, they would try to zoom past the officer (Smokey in trucker vernacular) with enough speed and closeness to "blow Smokey's hat off."

Well, not only is this sport rather disrespectful of law enforcement, but it is downright dangerous as well. To put a stop to this, states instituted new laws that required drivers to move over when they happened upon an officer and cruiser pulled off the road, doing their duty.

These laws are now called the "move over" laws.

So when Officer Buford pulled his hat and head from the Corolla, a car speeding more than a hundred miles per hour zoomed past close enough and with enough speed to "blow Smokey's hat off."

But wait. There're more.

The speeding—and no doubt drunken yahoos—threw an empty beer can at Deputy Buford for good measure. Deputy Buford scrambled to retrieve his hat, and in full fury, yelled at TJ and Rajah that he would attend to them later. He then raced back to his Ford V-8 Interceptor, and with his police chops licking, was fully excited that he was going to embark on a full-scale, high-speed highway pursuit.

Officer Buford was now on a real mission, and he had a lawful duty to overcome any physical shortcomings that may have restrained him during normal activities. The angry deputy jumped into his cruiser, buckled his 3-point seat belt, slapped his pointy toe boot to the metal, and with the mighty belch fire V-8 roaring, spun out from behind the little brown Corolla.

Well, bad things can happen when experienced NASCAR drivers apply too much power to their race cars, and so too, bad things can happen when a righteous but inexperienced deputy applies too much power to his Interceptor in the attempt to catch speeding bad guys. Deputy Buford spun out in some gravel while leaving the Corolla behind and hit the hard payment with the cruiser sideways to the intended point of travel. With justice on his side, the deputy did not back off.

Oh no, with pointy toe jabbing at the metal of the floor pan, the V-8 engine faithfully remained committed to applying full power to the spinning rear wheels.

The spinning rear wheels of the Interceptor was contributing to the fishtailing motion on the highway, that in turn was aided and abetted by the jerking of the steering wheel back and forth by a furious officer of the law. Unfortunately, intercepting the speeding bad guys would have to wait for another day because Officer Buford, still jerking at the wheel, slammed straight into an old growth oak tree of considerable girth.

TJ and Rajah were frozen in their seats as they witnessed what just happened. The horrible thud of the Interceptor crashing against the tree blocked out any bad feelings they had been harboring for Officer Buford.

The boys in the Corolla did what all good and normal people do. They rushed to the aid of Officer Buford. What they saw when they got to the wrecked Interceptor turned their stomachs. Officer Buford was bloodied, and his right arm was clearly broken. As the boys prepared to render aid, they witnessed Officer Buford use his left hand to pull his sidearm from its holster. Not knowing if Officer Buford was intending to shoot them, TJ and Rajah stepped back, confused and not knowing what next to do.

Confusion and astonishment reigned as TJ and Rajah witnessed in fascinated horror as Officer Buford, with fire in his eyes, managed to get his Glock 40 into his right hand. That is, the right hand of the broken right arm. Officer Buford managed to point the weapon out the open window and into the general direction of the speeding bad guys. In an instant TJ and Rajah knew that Officer Buford was intending to light off a 40mm round from his Glock 40 sidearm in the general direction of the speeding vehicle.

TJ and Rajah at once began shouting at the top of their lungs, "Don't shoot, Officer. Don't shoot. Don't shoot."

Officer Buford did not hear their warning, and he managed somehow to pull the trigger of his sidearm.

The kick from his gun was substantial enough to force the broken arm to splinter further, causing unimaginable pain. The bellowing scream from Officer Buford chilled their blood. The memory of the Officer's agony would be seared into TJ and Rajah's brains for as long as they lived.

Fortunately, after the shock of the weapon firing, Officer Buford dropped the gun, thus preventing any further danger. The intense pain also caused Office Buford to lose consciousness, leaving the boys once again not knowing what to do next.

Rajah finally corralled his thoughts enough to yell to TJ, "Call 911. Call 911."

TJ called 911 and told the person answering to stop asking a million dumb-ass questions and send an ambulance at once because an officer was down.

TJ hung up on the 911 Operator in total disgust so that he and Rajah could render immediate aid to Officer Buford. They searched for all of the bleeders that were visible and applied pressure to each area to control as much bleeding as possible. They then covered the deputy with a blanket they got from their car. They were aware shock would set in, and there was an urgent need to preserve as much body heat as possible.

They waited patiently for the ambulance to arrive, which came only after an entire platoon of police cars first had arrived. When a call "Officer down" goes out, the response from all police organizations in the vicinity is immediate.

After some tense moments during which the arriving police tried to determine if the boys were perpetrators, they split up and rushed to chase the speeding bad guys who had started the whole chain of events.

TJ and Rajah were eventually released with instructions to remain available for further questioning should it became necessary. Deputy Sheriff Buford would eventually recover enough to drive a desk in a regional headquarters instead of an Interceptor on the open road for the rest of his natural born policing career.

The speeding yahoos who blew Smokey's hat off were caught when the SUV they were driving spun out of control and came to rest in a ditch. One can only speculate as to the extent of the punishment the state was preparing to divvy out to the drunken thrill seekers.

During a quiet moment that the two spent reflecting upon the recent highway events, Rajah concluded there was certainly never a dull moment hanging with TJ. *Well*, thought the math wiz, *I will not be bored, even though I may end up in jail.* Mr. and Mrs. Barnabas were not at all pleased or amused that their genius son was wasting his precious life hanging with the likes of one Thaddeus Jones.

TJ thought the episode conclusively proved how dumb and out of control the state really was with its endless dogmatic laws and the ubiquitous police powers to enforce them.

CHAPTER 6

It Sure Took 1984 a Long Time to Get Here

The Jones's basement was fast becoming a place of refuge as well as a place for weighty discussions. Perhaps it was the closed-in, musty, and dank smell that marked their place as special when they removed themselves from the normal social chatter and babble of the spacious outside world. During quiet moments both TJ and Rajah lazily watched the specs of dust floating by on the beams of light coming from the dirty basement window. Those specs of dust reminded the both of them that they, too, were just specs of humanity floating by on beams of indifference coming from a dirty window of a busy world that cared little what was going on in a Marcus Cicero inspired basement.

Lately, TJ and Rajah spent most of their idle hours in the basement, dissecting and analyzing the events associated with Officer Buford and their run-in with the law. Both young patriots agreed that the most disturbing and unanticipated result of the episode was the loss of control over their own lives they felt when the state in the form of a uniformed policeman exercised its power over its citizens.

Not only that, but they had both experienced abject fear during the encounter and noted how that fear changed their focus from indignant and righteous citizens to human animals with a heightened instinct for survival.

Both agreed that they had not considered fear as a control motivator, even though their extensive education had made clear that despots and tyrannical governments had all used fear of the police and other governmental powers to enforce the desired behavior of its citizens.

Upon further consideration, both TJ and Rajah began to speculate as to what a modern state could do to generate fear to force desired behavior. It occurred to both of them that the possibility of governmental-manufactured fear could be just as effective in that regard as real existential (police) fear.

With a bolt of understanding, TJ and Rajah realized that by utilizing the science of psychology, people could employ a new and improved twenty-first-century way to efficiently produce targeted fear by means of psychologically directed thought control.

Thought control is one of the most efficient producers of fear. When properly executed by the government, the people themselves will become an all-encompassing existential police force that can wield ubiquitous fear through peer pressure so that everyone conforms to the correct thoughts.

Chairman Mao Zedong perfected this method of thought control, and the youth of China responded by forming the Red Guard to police and enforce the program. So in reality, government thought control is not just a theory. It has already been done on a very large scale in China as well as the USSR.

The employment of governmental thought control, therefore, becomes a very efficient way to advance political power. People can use the fear generated by the people themselves to pressure people into conforming to the government's will. This winning formula also produces little likelihood of a people's democratic reprisal.

Oh, my God, have we just described today's political correctness?

Modern technology now affords the government an unlimited opportunity for thought control through the use of mass media, academia, and other government-funded opinion makers. In fact, the message can often seem to spring forth from the people themselves.

Using the additional power of taxes, paid-for professional politicians, and many other governmental means can make a well-designed government program based on thought control viable and effective beyond mere mortals understanding.

The point being, studying the state's use of fear and experiencing fear in a real-life setting brought knowledge to the table that books and professors could never have given to them.

And furthermore, they were just single young men with hardly a care in the world. What if they had a family to protect? Wouldn't having a wife, children, property, and a job to protect make you even more venerable to the use of fear?

All of a sudden, both TJ and Rajah came to the same realization at the same time. The government and its highly educated minions could even encourage the establishment of families in order to force multiply the controlling factor of fear.

TJ and Rajah looked each other squarely in the eyes and said, "No, no, not our United States of America. Our government could never be that insidious in its lust for power."

Of course, they knew that all governments, by their political nature, were insidious and would indeed use every device and method at their disposal to maintain and gain power. However, TJ and Rajah steadfastly refused to believe that our government "of the people, by the people, and for the people" would ever dishonor our final trust by doing such a thing.

Dishonor or not, TJ was quick to point out that historically, governments have used religion for this very purpose ever since mankind learned to speak, so using families for the same purpose would require even less effort, and this manipulation would also be nearly invisible.

Rajah felt like a lost child with all of this talk about insidious governments, and so with a despondent sigh, he rejoined, "TJ, we are just now getting our lives in order after a rather rocky start in school and university with all of your kibitzing and all of my impatience with incompetent tenured math professors. I have a really great opportunity to join the research team at Global Technologies, and you have finally secured a decent position at Ubiquitous Insurance Underwriters. And here we are trying to change the world after getting our pants scared off by a big-belly sheriff patrolling the cornfields of nowhere Indiana."

Rajah continued, "What I'm trying to get my mind around is the fact that the world is a really big place with enough moving parts to cause a room full of Cray computers to burn up trying to make sense of it all. And here we are—two idealistic and wide-eyed kids trying to make a real difference. It's like we are trying to move the moon with a really long and wobbly stick."

Rajah finished by saying, "Well, as usually, the case, high purpose, and your need for daily bread are often at odds with one another."

While the contrarian and nerd contemplated the fear factor and the daily need for bread, something was beginning to stir in a world far, far away from where TJ and Rajah ate and slept. In the far away world little wheels began to turn that were causing more even more wheels to turn in that great big government machine.

What is causing all of these wheels to begin turning in the heart of a government machine that is, for the most part, insensitive to mere citizen?

Perhaps some context would be helpful.

In recent years, a populistic metaphor called the butterfly effect has sprung into common usage. Reference to the butterfly effect came into popular usage because of a movie that had the term as its title. However, the term has some real meaning in a scientific sense, even though the movie appropriated the real meaning and turned it into a cause celebre concerning human activity. In short, sometimes an innocuous and seemingly unrelated human action can cause a cascade of events that ends up bringing about a very large and oftentimes disastrous reaction.

The butterfly effect is so named because of the very unscientific notion that the beating of a single butterfly's wings in the correct place at the correct time can cause a cascade of meteorological events resulting in the creation of a hurricane at a later time and distant place. All in all, the butterfly effect is a fanciful and satisfying notion that can help explain the unexplainable to a person who might well be confounded by seemly unrelated events.

The term, however, has a real scientific basis in chaos theory. The butterfly effect is the sensitive dependence on initial conditions in which a small change in one state of a deterministic nonlinear system can result in large differences in a later state.

You can count on Hollywood to render complex scientific theory down into pulp fiction.

Well, it seems that the butterfly effect is real enough to manifest its force in the real world of our two happy-go-lucky patriots. The purpose-driven world that TJ and Rajah are now enjoying had already begun to change because of an insignificant highway adventure with Officer Buford and their impulsive speaking at a government-sponsored symposium about man-caused climate change.

Two butterfly patriots beating their insignificant yaps at the correct place and at the correct time was beginning to cause a cascade of events that would lead to the creation of governmental hurricane. Somewhere in the bowels of our government, where people think about how to expand and conserve government power, concern was developing. It seemed that support for the government's latest power grab was waning.

The power grab was part of the globalist's movement that has eagerly adopted global climate change as a crisis to take advantage of. The power grab is one that is designed to give the appearance that the new government control over vast areas of the country's economy is the only way to save the planet from an environmental disaster caused by unbridled human activity.

You know the story by now.

The evil raping of the environment by human activity is causing the uncontrolled warming of planet Earth. The uncontrolled warming is, thereby, resulting in a catastrophic climate change that will destroy gracious Mother Earth as we know it. And only a ubiquitous world government will have enough power to rein in and control all of humankind's activity and thereby save us all.

The power grab is designed to empower and encourage well-meaning and gullible citizens to embrace the government takeover in order to utilize citizen peer pressure to ridicule and demean those freedom lovers who take exception to the governmental takeover of so much of the country's economy.

To aid and abet the thought control program, the government will use the treasury to fund only the scientists and entities that support the government takeover. The largess of the public treasury will assure enthusiastic and seemingly ubiquitous support from all corners of "knowledgeable" thought.

But who on earth can be against the government saving Mother Earth for us all?

Never mind that prior to the "scientific" fact that human activity is causing uncontrolled warming of the environment, most of the scientific community supported the "scientific" fact that a new ice age would soon descend upon us. Rational people can only speculate how a slight global warming, if it is real, can be more harmful than a mile thick ice sheet over our heads.

Indeed, warming periods have been the key enabling events that promote human advancement because of the reduced need to spend all of our efforts just to eat and survive in an inhospitable environment. It is more than ironic that the current warming event (if it really exists because of human activity) has also enabled the arts and finer aspects of our social existence to expand and is now being demonized as a danger to us all.

There is little doubt that rational people of all strips and colors would soon realize that if an impending ice age was selected as the vehicle for a new global governmental power grab instead of global warming, the same program of thought control would be use to enable complete governmental control over the economy and all human activity. A global governmental control program would be crafted and spun as the only way to save us all from certain ruin by an impending new ice age.

So the government deep thinkers addressed the issue of waning support for the global warming cause celebre, now changed to climate change, and after endless discussions, they issued that all-powerful governmental instrument known as a memorandum of understanding (MOU).

The MOU was quickly classified top secret so that nosey citizens would not become privy to what their government was up to. The MOU suggested the best way to shore up citizen support of governmental control over the economy was to prosecute the

climate change deniers under the Racketeer Influenced and
Corrupt Organizations Act (RICO). Perhaps this has something
to do with instilling fear in order to facilitate desired activity.

The deep thinkers thought they could do this now that a
successful governmental prosecution of the tobacco industry had
been carried out in the past. After all, the tobacco industry had
denied the scientific settled fact of tobacco's harm to human
health.

And because the climate change deniers were also deniers
of the settled scientific fact of human-caused climate change, a
successful prosecution of a selected climate change denier under
the RICO Act would ensure that the great motivator, fear, could
be efficiently utilized to curtail any further dissent.

The MOU was disseminated to all of the appropriate
governmental agencies along with a White House admonition
to quickly design the means to implement the MOU
recommendations. Needless to say, all government pooh-bahs and
apparatchiks promptly fell in line with the White House direction
and soon brought forth another very powerful governmental
instrument called a memorandum of agreement (MOA). A MOA
details the means to comply with the recommendations of the
MOU.

Wheels and wheels within wheels were all now turning in
perfect bureaucratic syncopation assuring that swift and decisive
government action would instill fear in all those who has the
audacity to defy governmental authority and power. These
missions involving the application of government power and
authority are vital if the government is to maintain its control
over the people.

With the MOU and MOA in full force, it was decided that
the Justice Department would prosecute the selected climate
change denier under the RICO Act. Much discussion ensued,

but who the recipients of the Justice Department's prosecution would be was never really in doubt.

The selected climate change denier would have to be a citizen at large because the idea was to instill fear in the movers/shakers, not prosecute them. God only knows when the government might need the movers/shakers to do a service for them, and so wise authorities should not knowingly piss off the movers/shakers by actually prosecuting them.

Sort of sounds like what Vito Corleone said in *The Godfather*, doesn't it?

If you would like to see this governmental paradigm in action, you can watch the Australian film *Breaker Morant* for real life and reality.

The film *Breaker Morant* details how England facilitated the end of the Boer War. England decided to prosecute someone for war crimes in order to assure the Boers that England did indeed want to end the conflict. England wanted to end the conflict in such a manner to provide both parties with some gains that were beneficial to all. It was decided to prosecute some unwitting Australians soldiers because England could claim the Australians soldiers had gone rogue in the conflict and had caused undue harm upon the Boers.

And so England would prosecute the rogue soldiers to prove to the Boers and the world that England was a country invested in justice. England selected Breaker Morant and his lieutenant to be the scapegoats in this nefarious undertaking. The Australian government agreed to this unjust arrangement in order to prevent any further Australian personnel losses.

In like manner, the US Justice Department would select a citizen at large to be the scapegoat in the prosecution of climate change deniers in order to shore up support for the government

Ronald L. Clark

power grab over the economy without pissing off the mover/shakes.

First up would be the attorney general setting up a press conference to announce to the world and citizens at large that the Justice Department was in the process of deciding to prosecute climate change deniers under the RICO Act. The government wanted to send a message that deniers of the scientific-settled fact of man-caused climate change would no longer be tolerated.

Bear in mind that this prosecution was intended to instill fear. Climate change deniers were not in any way prohibiting the government from proceeding with its program of economy takeover in order to save the planet from man-caused climate change.

To think the government—any government—could actually control the climate of planet Earth is stupefying beyond any rational belief. However, rational cognition is not a functional aspect of any government that can only make decisions based on political constraints and endeavors.

So therefore a political wind of sizable proportions began to blow up a blizzard of bureaucratic memos that blew in from Apparatchik Central and blanketed the multitude of offices of your government with actionable items to facilitate implantation the MOU and MOA.

That is, when the attorney general supposes, bureaucratic minions begin to propose things. As the multitude of governmental wheels began to spin, they in turn spew forth even more proposals. Those little functional wheels rattle into action to prove their worth and churn out suggested actionable items (AIs) to feed the hungry government beast.

And as is the case with the human adventure, strange and seemingly unrelated things somehow coalesced by some unknown mysterious force and produced just another actionable item.

However, this particular actionable item (AI) joined the river of other actionable items that was infusing the levers of governmental power with decision-making fodder.

The unknown forces that brought this peculiar actionable item into being are as mysterious as the random forces that brought forth life on Mother Earth.

Once again, somehow some sort of symmetry has been achieved here.

Regardless, an actionable item that was flowing in the river of actionable items came to the attention of just another governmental apparatchik.

This particular apparatchik knew a golden opportunity when he saw it, and he seized upon the peculiar actionable item as an opportunity to advance into the upper stratum of government power by providing just what the attorney general needed.

And further, being an accomplished apparatchik, he knew just what to do with the actionable item that the innocuous little functional wheel of the government had produced. First off, the innocuous functional wheel was given official praise in the form of an Atta Boy from apparatchik heaven, thereby releasing the innocuous wheel from any further connection with the actionable item in question.

The apparatchik took complete ownership of the cherished actionable item and dismissed the innocuous little wheel back into obscurity where he belonged. Now that the actionable item was firmly under his control, the apparatchik began the process of constructing the legal and operational framework to aid in the prosecution of the selected climate change denier. In this case, it was two citizen climate change deniers that the AI had stumbled upon during the course of his official duties.

And most importantly, the accomplished apparatchik had to create the means for "creditable deniability" for the at risk politicial appointees in the unlikely event that the prosecution Choo Choo flew off its tracks and someone had to be sacrificed.

Creditable deniability is the Holy Grail for preserving upper-level political appointees from ever suffering the slings and arrows of failure and being held accountable for anything politically unpleasant.

The actionable item produced by the innocuous government wheel was an admirable happenstance. The little wheel wanted to hear what was being said at a seminar on climate change at the local university in his district, and of all things, there were two citizen climate change deniers raising voice against the government and the settled science on the matter.

You know, the TJ and Rajah who were ridiculing the university-sponsored notion that farting cows were sending us all down into climate Armageddon.

This strange and seemingly unrelated event of two rather young contrarians taking issue with their government at a university seminar, and an obscure government official killing time at the same seminar, is the stuff of movies. You know, the butterfly effect in action.

However, like the old saying states, "Chance favors the prepared," and that attitude was present here in this nefarious happenstance. The government wheel took note of the climate change deniers expressing their skepticism, not so much about the substance of their disagreement but rather the fact that they were engaged in open opposition. So this chance occurrence prompted the ever-vigilant little wheel to obtain the names of the climate change deniers before he departed the seminar—Thaddeus Jones and Roger Barnabas.

And because the little wheel didn't have much meaningful work to do, he spent a great deal of time reading official government memos. And as luck would have it, the ever-prepared little wheel read the memo concerning the hunt for citizen candidates for prosecution under the RICO Act for the hideous crime of denying climate change.

Alarm bells sounded. Lighting flashed. Klaxons began growling, and all of the neurons fired and synapses connected away in the brain of the little government official as he scored with the match of the recorded names of Thaddeus Jones and Roger Barnabas and the need for citizen climate change deniers. These guys could just be what the Justice Department needed for the federal prosecution of climate change deniers. The official got so excited at the prospect of being recognized by his higher-ups that he had to make an unscheduled pit stop at the urinal to relive the excitement. After things calmed down a bit, the little wheel thought it would be wise to run the names of Thaddeus Jones and Roger Barnabas through the extensive database of the US government.

The results of the search was so stunning that he had to make another pit stop in order to keep from embarrassing himself in front of the other government officials hard at work reading government memos at their workstations.

According to the integrated government database, one Thaddeus Jones and one Roger Barnabas had been involved in a highway incident that implicated them in not only a violation of traffic laws but also substantial disrespect for law enforcement. The incident further included a deputy sheriff suffering injuries under suspicious circumstances and the eventual crash of another vehicle with four drunken yahoos on holiday.

The fortuitous data dump sent chills down the leg of the government official as he realized that the climate deniers not only were lawbreakers but may have contributed to the serious injury of a uniformed law officer as well. These *facts* were more than enough to cement their candidacy for use by the Justice Department.

After the official transmitted all of the incriminating *facts*, his duty apparatchik gave forth with a glowing approval and forwarded the candidate dossier to all associated governmental apparatchiks.

After endless meetings by unknown numbers of lawyers, department heads, political operatives, and God only knows who else, unanimous approval was granted, and a recommendation to proceed was forwarded to the office of the attorney general.

To say the office of the attorney general was pleased with the efforts of the governmental bureaucracy would be an understatement of epic proportions.

CHAPTER 7

Farting Cows Will Lead Us All to Climate Armageddon

TJ was sitting at the kitchen table, having coffee and sharing conversation with his parents, Mom and Pop Jones. The delicious aroma of toasted cinnamon bread and freshly brewed coffee wafted throughout the kitchen and made just the right atmosphere for a relaxed and congenital family sit down.

The Russians say that all really important matters are discussed and decided at the kitchen table, and perhaps the Russian proverb is rather accurate. During the family conversation about family matters, work, school, social faux pas, girlfriends, among other things, the Jones's doorbell rang with unusual authority.

Pop Jones slowly rose with a geezer groan and went to the door only to discover a very stern-looking fellow in a issue quality dark suit standing there with an impatient stance. Pop Jones looked past the statue of a man and saw a big black Suburban parked in his driveway, the motor still running. Needless to say, Pop Jones became apprehensive and concerned all at the same time.

The very tall and statuette man was not only clad in a black suit that would have made the Blues Brothers proud, but his black shoes were also shined to a mirror finish that would pass any marine inspection. His extraordinarily wide shoulders made him look like a Colt's running back. The suit could not hide a suspicious bulge under his left lapel.

And furthermore, there were the obligatory mirrored shades guarding his eyes. A wire stuck in the man's ear completed the entire ensemble.

The man in black looked straight through Pop Jones and announced in a surprisingly high-pitched voice, "My name is Agent Robrowski, I am an agent of the department of justice. Are you Thaddeus Jones?"

In a somewhat shaky voice, Pop Jones answered, "Oh yeah, and I'm Czar of Russia."

Statue man still looked through Pop, and with practiced and professional speed, yanked out a worn black leather scabbard festooned with a very large and shiny six-pointed star badge. There was also a picture of statue man with the words "United States of America Department of Justice, and Victor Robrowski."

Then statue man, still holding his badge at arm's length, barked, "Agent Robrowski, Department of Justice." He slipped his credentials back into his right breast pocket and then asked, "Where can I find Thaddeus Jones?"

Pop Jones replied, "Well, he is right here in the kitchen with his mother."

When statue man heard the word *mother*, he soften ever-so-slightly, and asked, "Would you please be so kind to ask Mr. Thaddeus Jones to please come to the door?"

Pop Jones's protectiveness kicked in, and he replied, "What business do you have with my son?"

Statue man replied in a slightly hushed and threatening voice, "Sir, I am only allowed to discuss that matter with Thaddeus Jones. Will you please ask him to come to the door?"

Pop Jones stood a little straighter and inquired, "What if Thaddeus elects not to come to the door?"

Statue man looked pleased with the question, flashed a knowing grin, and quickly said, "I have a lawful search warrant signed by a federal judge allowing me to force entry into your home in order to search for a Thaddeus Jones. Would you like to examine it?"

Pop Jones stepped back a bit when he heard the man's curt reply, turned, and mumbled toward the kitchen, "TJ, there is someone here who wants to speak with you."

TJ looked apprehensively at his mother and shrugged before heading off to the door. Upon seeing statue man standing there, TJ immediately had a flashback of Officer Buford standing outside his car in all of his grand authority.

TJ's knees buckled at the memory as he made his way to the door.

Before TJ could announce himself, the man barked, "Are you Thaddeus Jones?"

TJ could only answer, "Yes."

Agent Robrowski reached into a pouch hidden somewhere and pulled out an official-looking sheath of papers. Agent Robrowski opened the door and placed the papers into Thaddeus Jones's limp hand.

The agent then said in an authoritarian voice, "You have been served with a summons to appear at the stated office of the attorney general on the date and time listed. At that time and place, representatives of the US Department of Justice will interview you under oath. You may bring legal counsel if you so desire, but that counsel cannot participate in any way during the interview. Do you understand?"

TJ looked like a deer caught in headlights and mumbled, "Yes."

When he heard the affirmative from Thaddeus Jones, statue man wheeled about in a military manner, marched off down the sidewalk, and got into the waiting big black Suburban vehicle.

Agent Robrowski departed the premises, and it was as if he had never been there. This same summons was also being executed at the home of Mr. and Mrs. Barnabas, and at the same time and with the same precision by another agent who was every bit the equal of Agent Robrowski.

Rajah was standing in the doorway and looking out at the departing black Suburban. He stared down at the official government summons in his limp hand. Unknown and primitive forces were directing his reactions at this point. His attention was wavering back and forth between watching the departing black Suburban and gazing down intently at the summons. Roger Barnabas did not know what to do.

When the Suburban finally vanished to places unknown, nosey neighbors stared at the departing official government vehicle and the front door of the Barnabas house. The extraordinary event had the neighborhood inhabitants reacting in hushed chatter and darting eyes that rose in intensity and speed with each passing minute.

Texting, e-mails, tweets, snap chats, and phone calls ensured that lively conversation and conjecture would be running rampant for the foreseeable future in the previously boring Barnabas neighborhood.

As for Rajah, his mind was sucking up all available energy from his young physiology in an endeavor to ferret out some meaningful clues about what may have prompted such strange goings-on. Rajah's hand was also limp, and most other bodily functions were also flaccid. However, he felt an urgent need to go to the bathroom.

Mr. and Mrs. Barnabas nodded their heads, turned toward each other in a perfect synchronization that only twenty-five years of marriage could cultivate, and exclaimed in unison, "This is what comes from hanging out with the likes of Thaddeus Jones."

TJ and Rajah arrived on the appointed date at the scheduled time at the local federal office, where foreboding and all-powerful federal officials who answered to no one were waiting to *interview* the young men who could not yet figure out why they were in so much trouble with the Feds. To the best of their deliberations, nothing came to mind except the run-in with Officer Buford. However, they failed to see how that episode in an Indiana cornfield could possibly rise to the level of a federal offense.

Upon arrival, TJ and Rajah were spirited off to separate interview rooms so as to ensure that the two persons of interest could not coordinate their *facts* with winks, blinks, or nods. Good American citizens know that federal officials are only concerned with what is the truth, the whole truth, and nothing but the truth, so help them God. TJ and Rajah could not afford legal counsel, so they went into the interviews commando.

The fact-finding government interview was conducted in a room with a suspicious opaque glass covering most of a wall and a room full of imposing people of all sizes, shapes, and colors. The head interviewer said that the interview would be recorded.

With eyes wide open, TJ asked, "Will you be reading me my Miranda rights?"

The interviewing entourage all stifled an official chuckle at the innocent question, and when all had settled down, the head interviewer said, "No, you will not be given Miranda rights because we are the Department of Justice, and as such, we are not a police organization. We are not required to administer Miranda rights to criminal suspects."

TJ looked puzzled and asked, "So I am not a criminal suspect?"

The interviewer responded, "Of course not. We are the Department of Justice, and as such, we are only conducting a fact-finding interview to determine if the facts discovered during this interview warrant forwarding them to the prosecuting section of the Justice Department for criminal prosecution in a federal court."

TJ's butt hole cinched up again. Tense or not, the contrarian force kicked in for TJ, and he then responded, "So if I am not a criminal suspect in a criminal investigation, then am I free to leave?"

The interviewer squirmed ever-so-slightly in his chair, cleared his throat, and said with a deep voice, "See that big fellow over there by the door? I am referring to the fellow with a black suit on and with a firearm on his hip. Well, that gentleman is a federal marshal, and if you try to leave this interview, he is authorized to take you into custody for failure to cooperate with a federal official."

TJ looked at the imposing federal marshal, turned to the interviewer, and asked, "What happens when I am taken into custody?"

The interviewer quickly responded, "You will be taken before a federal judge who will then remand you to a federal detention facility until you are ready to cooperate with the federal official sitting before you."

TJ paused to carefully think over what had just been said. He then looked the interviewer straight in the eye and said, "So if I were a criminal, I would have Miranda rights to remain silent, but as an innocent citizen, I have no such rights, correct?"

The interviewer waved to the assembled federal entourage and lightheartedly exclaimed, "Will you listen to this young man? You would think that he is interviewing us. Wow, that's rich. Well now, Mr. Jones, I can assure you that the Department of Justice personnel assembled here today are only here to participate in a fact-finding interview with you, and as such, your constitutional rights as a citizen of the United States of America will always be fully considered."

The government entourage all nodded in positive unison.

TJ laughed out loud at this BS and said, "Let me see if I have this correct. You are going to record the interview with me, and for what purpose? If I were a criminal suspect given Miranda rights, you would tell me that everything I say can and will be held against me in a court of law. In addition, Miranda rights also state that the criminal suspect has the right to remain silent because he cannot be forced to incriminate himself. However, because I am not a criminal suspect with Miranda rights, I must cooperate with an authorized federal office or be carted off to jail until I do cooperate. Further, because my interview will be recorded, there will be a record if I lie or misrepresent the facts according to government interpretation of those facts. Lying to a government official is a federal crime, and off to jail I go. Interpreting the facts that are in conflict with the government interpretation provides the means for all kinds of government mischief. Sure sounds like to me that I can be forced to incriminate myself in a manner authorized by the government."

The assembled government automatons all fell silent. All bureaucrats instinctively know when it's time to not speak up. This is the time to let the head automaton earn his keep.

But before the interviewer could respond, TJ continued, "And further, because I am not a criminal suspect, I am not allowed to have legal counsel present to participate in this proceeding. That being the reality of this situation means my constitutional rights can only be protected during this interview by the government officials assembled here, all of whom are ready to prosecute me at the slightest federal infraction. Needless to say, I know a stacked deck when I see one."

In a practiced and patronizing manner, the interviewer finally spoke up and said, "Now, now, Mr. Jones, you know full well you have the ability to sue the federal government in federal court should you feel your constitutional rights have been violated."

All of the government automatons suppressed a knowing chuckle at the mere suggestion that the federal juggernaut could ever be brought to heel in a federal court of law by an unconnected US citizen of modest means, especially if he was not one of the protected minorities.

The interviewer continued, "The reason we must record the interview is to protect you from something being stated that you did not say. In other words, the recording is solely intended to accurately record the facts as they are stated by all parties."

TJ was beginning to feel the effects of mental exhaustion brought about by inability to affect any aspect of his current circumstance. In frustration, TJ exclaimed, "Hell, I still don't even know why you forced me to come here."

A satisfied hush fell over the government side because they knew the dam of resistance had finally been broken, and so they could finally get down to business now.

The interviewer shuffled his papers in another practiced move to promote the appearance of power, looked up with lifeless eyes at the pathetic and powerless citizen seated before him, and then slowly gazed at each and every one of the assembled government officials to assure them all that he was fully in charge. He then picked up a number of official papers, looked at the papers as if he had just seen them, and with demonstrated authority, proclaimed with perfect diction, "What I have before me is a police report concerning you and a Mr. Roger Barnabas."

The interviewer paused for effect and then proceeded, "This police report details all of the circumstances that began when you, Thaddeus Jones, were operating a motor vehicle that Officer Buford observed violating a traffic law. Officer Buford then affected a highway traffic stop in order to issue a citation for the observed traffic violation. Details concerning the lawful traffic stop indicate a subsequence series of events that resulted in the serious wounding of an officer of the law."

Again, the interviewer paused long enough for the significance of the statement to fully sink in. Then he carefully straighten the police report papers, paused as if to consider something profound, and continued, "While the details of the incident does not warrant further federal government action, what this report clearly shows is that Thaddeus Jones and Roger Barnabas demonstrated a lack of respect for not only the law but for lawful officers as well. The fact is that Thaddeus Jones, by violating traffic laws and disrespecting a law enforcement officer, started the chain of events that culminated in the serious wounding of a police officer. Therefore, Thaddeus Jones and Roger Barnabas must share a measure of responsibility for the wounding of Officer Buford. This in itself is a very serious matter, but what it also shows is that Thaddeus Jones and Roger Barnabas have shown a pattern of lawbreaking and disrespect for the law and law officers. This pattern is the basis for the inquiry into the events surrounding a confrontation between Thaddeus Jones and an esteemed professor giving a seminar on man-caused climate change."

The interviewer carefully placed the police papers down and looked at Thaddeus Jones, who had a bewildered look on his face now. He couldn't believe what the interviewer had just said.

TJ mumbled to no one in particular, "Holy shit. Are you telling me farting cows is what got me in trouble with the Feds?"

Completely ignoring TJ, the interviewer shuffled through his stack of papers until he found what he was looking for. He carefully arranged the selected papers into the order he wanted and paused to make sure everyone was still paying attention to his carefully orchestrated moves. He selected the papers from the report of a minor government official who happened to attend the same seminar on global climate change that TJ and Rajah had attended.

The seminar on climate change was curious in many ways if one was interested enough to research how it originated. For example, the seminar was sponsored and paid for by the government. The government also funded the esteemed professor who presented the seminar. The professor was paid to research how humans were indeed causing climate change. Likewise, the university was the recipient of a very large block grant from the government to further any and all studies concerning how man was causing climate change. Further still, the government stipulated that it would no longer fund professors and their research if their research did not support the science of man-caused climate change. And moreover, the government informed the university that unrelated government support for university programs would also suffer if the regents did not actively support research that validated the scientific fact that man was indeed causing catastrophic climate change. Needless to say, university enthusiasm was overwhelming in its support of the scientifically settled question of man-caused climate change.

The interviewer once again cleared his throat to signify he was about to speak again. Looking intently at the selected papers about the seminar on climate change, he continued, "I have a report here that details how a Mr. Thaddeus Jones stood up during a presentation on man-caused climate change by an esteemed professor and interrupted the presentation by calling the professor and his findings 'an idiot and bullshit' accordingly."

The interviewer waited for the laughter to settle down before proceeding with his august reading of the happenings during the university seminar on climate change. The assembled entourage looked at the interviewer with a degree of admiration, and then they turned to the pathetic and powerless citizen squirming in the hot seat with a slight degree of sympathy. Nevertheless, the interviewer added to the record, "The professor, a civil and polite man, stopped his presentation to ask Mr. Jones about the basis for his accusation.

Whereupon Mr. Thaddeus Jones repudiated the professor by saying, 'Suppressed scientific fact states that CO_2 contributes less than 0.05 percent of the calculated heat trapping of the sun's radiated energy. And yet you say that CO_2 is what is causing the Earth's climate to rise and the government's need to control all things that emit CO_2. Notwithstanding that humans emit CO_2 when they exhale and that life-sustaining process is now deemed to be a pollutant that must come under complete government control. As a sidebar, who among us will speak for all things green that must have CO_2 in order to live and provide the basis for all life on the planet? And now you say that are vast herds of cattle roaming the Earth's surface and eating every green thing in sight which causes the cattle to emit copious amounts of flatulence in the form of methane, a more powerful heat-trapping gas than CO_2. By your very own words, Professor, farting cows will lead us all down to climate Armageddon. To prevent cows from farting, man must wean himself from meat eating in order to reduce the number of cows grazing upon the land and farting. So instead of eating meat, man must dine exclusively on plant life in order to save the planet. However, the solution of humans only eating plant life is a problem. Using the good professor's analysis, when humans begin to only eat green things, they, too, will increase their flatulence output (farting) and thereby be directly responsible for inundating Miami Beach with seawater.'"

Again, the interviewer had to restore order because of the laughter that the people could no longer contain. However, his stern looks reminded the government-paid serfs that this was no laughing matter.

The interviewer proceeded in a somber voice, "There are more of the same kind of exchanges between Mr. Jones and the eminent professor of Climatology, but in the interest of time, the exchange just stated is representative of the complete encounter between Mr. Jones and the professor. Now I ask you Mr. Thaddeus Jones, is the exchange I just presented, in fact true?"

Squirming, TJ sat up straight, looked at the assembly and the interviewer, and said, "Yep, that is exactly what I said. And further, what I said is the truth. So what?"

A very satisfied look softened the stern face of the interviewer when he responded with teeth slightly exposed in what some might say could have been the beginnings of a smile, "Thank you very much, Mr. Jones."

The interviewer set down the latest papers and began to search for more quotations in the last batch of official papers. When the search was complete, he sat up straight and said, "I now have before me transcripts of the various writings Mr. Jones has published in social media. These publications all have a common theme, and the message says that your government is not to be trusted and that all men are sovereign individuals and therefore are not bound to bend to their government's will."

The interviewer again turned to TJ and asked, "Mr. Jones, is what I presented concerning your social media publications correct?"

TJ answered the interviewer with a growing suspicion that this trouble with the Feds had more to do with government control than farting cows and out-of-control CO2. He said, "Well, sir, I will say your research into my behavior is spot on. I did publish what you said and will continue to do so in order to exercise my constitutional right of free speech."

The interviewer had finally gotten to the point. Now he could begin the task of summarizing his findings and the consequences of those findings in regards to Mr. Thaddeus Jones. He began, "Mr. Jones, when all of these events I have outlined here today are considered in their entirety, they clearly show that you have engaged in willful public obstruction of the government's lawful duty to address the serious issue of catastrophic climate change because of man's activity. You may think you have the right of free speech in order to repudiate the lawful government's ability to control key parts of human activity, but you do not. This issue has been adjudicated many times in federal court, and you may not do so without legal consequences. Just as the constitutional right of free speech does not allow you to yell, "Fire," in a crowded theater without there being a fire, you cannot engage in public repudiating of lawful governmental activity in order to serve it citizens without there being a factual reason to do so. In that regards, it is now a settled scientific fact that man's activities are causing catastrophic climate change, which will become harmful to the citizens. So it is settled that you do not have a factual reason to publicly repudiate the government's activity in trying to prevent catastrophic man-caused climate change.

"There is legal precedence already established in this regard. You may recall the successful government's legal action against the tobacco industry. The government litigated against the tobacco industry using the Racketeer Influenced and Corrupt Organizations Act. The government was successful in using this law because it was a settled scientific and medical fact that tobacco was harmful and injurious to public health. The tobacco industry was engaged in unlawful racketeering by using all manner of public instruments and public means along with discredited science in an attempt to repudiate a legitimate scientific fact and the government's lawful efforts to serve public health.

"The tobacco industry lost in federal court and faced serious legal consequences as a result. In like manner, if the Department of Justice determines that your public activities in relation to the settled scientific fact of man-caused climate change and the lawful government actions to serve its citizens, have risen to the level of RICO concerns, you may indeed face government litigation in a federal court of law."

The interviewer again paused after his department pronouncements, all of which had been vetted by hoards of government lawyers, to let what he had outlined sink in. After the appropriate delay, he then turned to TJ and asked, "Is there anything you would like to say?"

TJ's head was spinning after all of the legal mumbo jumbo. He squirmed, but then he figured, *Ah, what the hell! Nothing I can say will make one iota of difference to the government automatons, so I might as well just toss out my observations on the record.*

"Interview? You call these proceedings an interview? I know an inquisition when I see it. I now know how Galileo must have felt when he faced a similar *interview* by a Roman Catholic inquisition. I have nothing further to say."

The interviewer summarily closed the proceedings after informing Mr. Jones that he was not to leave the country, and to that end, he had to surrender his passport forthwith. In addition, he had to inform an agent of the Justice Department of his whereabouts at all times until the Department of Justice decided to proceed or drop the matter.

Mr. Roger Barnabas suffered the same fate as Mr. Thaddeus Jones, and in like manner, it was determined that he had aided and abetted the unlawful activities of Mr. Thaddeus Jones. Mr. and Mrs. Barnabas both said again, "This is what comes from hanging out with the likes of Thaddeus Jones."

The government case proceeded in accordance with the wishes of the attorney general with the full support from the White House. The two pathetic and powerless patriots who dared to think they could move the government juggernaut with a long and wobbly citizen stick would have to serve as examples to all others who dared to think they could obstruct their entrenched government.

TJ and Rajah both served time in the federal big house, thereby ending their lives as they knew them. Their sacred mission was stopped dead in its tracks before anyone even knew it existed.

They now knew the real power of their government of the people, by the people, and for the people.

All of this brings to mind the real life and times of Lt. Harry "Breaker" Morant as the English government sought to end the Boer war by unjustly executing two pathetic and powerless Australian soldiers who were in service to the crown.

We don't know the last words of TJ and Rajah, but Morant summed it very well by saying, "Shoot straight, you bastards. Don't make a mess of it."

The recipients of his pathetic directive were his fellow comrades in arms who were standing in formation, waiting for the sun to rise in order to follow their orders to execute their former leader.

After Lt. Harry "Breaker" Morant barked his last order to shoot straight, he turned to his condemned fellow Peter Handcock and said, "Well, Peter, this is what comes of empire building."

And so too, this is what comes of being a rock in a tree.

AFTERWORD

The new nobility we speak of here is the modern equivalent of the nobility that supported feudalism during the agricultural age. The new nobility is the self appointed and self-righteous oligarchy that is determined to advance the idea of a utopia in the information age The Neonobility Oligarchy will facilitate this idea because they feel they are the only ones that are smart enough to do so. Neonobility will use peer pressure brought about by the application of thought control enabled by a program of politicial correctness.

Neonobility

Fervent concern for fellow man
Self-righteously spews forth
With endless and boundless energy
To wrap itself around the perceived hapless
Who are trapped by the opiate of freedom
Into an addiction of personal liberty
That forces the hapless unenlightened to live
A life of unrestrained happiness.

Such selfish and boorish behavior cannot be long endured
By the cadre of self-appointed guardians for social justice.
So behold
A new age and enlightened army of social aristocracy
Marching into battle armed with laws, rules, regulations,
And the ultimate device of new age social weaponry,
Ubiquitous peer pressure
To engage the freedom-loving, unenlightened rabble
Into a perpetual war to ensure social justice for fellow man.

Liberty and personal freedom must bend
To the demands of the battle-tested concerned
Because only they know what is best and just for all
As they wage social war to finally usher in the Age of Aquarius
To finally bring forth the ultimate new age utopia
Where we all will live in peace and harmony.

Ushered in not from the barrel of a gun
But from the cannons of
Smothering government nudging
This being new and improved way
To change the nature of man
Into a malleable social instrument
To finally construct the new Age of Aquarius.

This then is the imperative that fuels the enlightened soul
To fashion a new and improved world
For the annals of human history
To celebrate their wisdom and concern
In bringing the elusive utopia
To the huddled masses
That also brings unto the noble effort
A flattering expansion of self-worth that the ego
Embraces with each self-righteous, altruistic blow delivered
Upon the proclaimed hapless, the ignorant, the boorish,
And the freedom-loving, selfish rabble
And huddled masses longing to be free.

And when united with fellow enlightened social warriors
Brings forth a shining and consecrated army
To wage social war
Upon the selfish, unenlightened hordes
And brings forth onto each
Individual enlightened and self-righteous warrior
The majestic providence of *power*,
Power that force the individual holy endeavors
Into an unstoppable progressive force
While satisfying a waxing addition to *power*
Even more forceful than gold had over Midas.

And because all humans are born
With a DNA-encoded lust for power,
Lesser man will always find a way
To satisfy that lust for power
Made all the better by exercising
More, more, and more *power*
For the betterment of all.

Now consider the poor, hapless individuals who are the recipients
Of the slings and arrows of the enlightened social holy war.
They are as unprotected as wayward sheep
Meandering into a pack of hungry wolves,
Righteous wolves made powerful by usurping government force
To stampede the leaderless rabble into the loving embrace
Of the social warrior wolves
Who always know what is best and just for us all.

So the unenlightened are constantly battered by the weapons
Of laws, rules, regulations, and manufactured peer pressure
That the holy social warriors use to grind down a person's dignity
Until the freedom-loving are forced to be constantly at odds
With their fellow man.
Indeed,
They are made to be outcasts within the community of man
And thereby made irreverent.

These are the consequences of being an independent
And a free soul nowadays in the land of government-supported
Holy social warriors forcing man to change
His nature to suit the enlightened mandate for a new age utopia
Where the splendid government
Of the people
By the people
For the people
So eloquently articulated by
President Abraham Lincoln

Only exists today within the echo
Of those magnificent words
That was sanctified by
The blood of fallen brethren
Upon a horrific hometown battlefield.

Pray tell,
Where is the today's eloquent president
Who will offer inspiring and comforting
Words over a battlefield,
Not one littered with broken bodies
But a modern battlefield littered with broken
Human dignity and freedom

Where only the ghosts of patriots past
Mingle with put-upon patriots of today
Once again seeking
To preserve, protect, and defend a splendid government
Of the people
By the people
For the people?

And pray tell,
Where are today's free citizens?
Those willing to sacrifice comfort, treasure, and life
In the endless struggle
To dignify and preserve freedom-endowed man?

Only the ghosts of patriots past
Cry out today for freedom and liberty,
Ghosts whose frail voices are
Only heard by a declining few
Battered by the united force of progressive thought
That exiles old-age man from the shining new age utopia,
Wailing with forlorn and pitiful weak voices,
Still crying out,
"Oh, Freedom, where art thou?"
Where even today
Feeble and frail voices are
Are still crying out,
"Oh, Freedom, where art thou?"

This is the pitiful cry
From today's battered patriots,
Battered and ridiculed
By the forces by ubiquitous concern
As the new age nobility swagger
And point a self-righteous finger toward
The sovereign man.

Printed in the United States
By Bookmasters